THE MEASURE OF THE WORLD

OTHER TITLES BY CHARLES DAVIS

Hitler, Mussolini, and Me

Standing at the Crossroads

Walk On, Bright Boy

Walking the Dog

Charles Davis

THE MEASURE OF THE WORLD

THE PERMANENT PRESS
Sag Harbor, NY 11963

For information, address:
  The Permanent Press
  4170 Noyac Road
  Sag Harbor, NY 11963
  www.thepermanentpress.com

Library of Congress Cataloging-in-Publication Data

  Davis, Charles, author.
    The measure of the world / Charles Davis.
    Sag Harbor, NY: The Permanent Press, 2019.
    ISBN: 978-1-57962-570-2

  PR6104.A88 M43 2019
  823'.92—dc23   2018057797

Printed in the United States of America

For Jeannette and a few more mountaintops

At eighteen, I was, like many young men, almost an imbecile, but I was plucky and did not defer to my handicap. Lunacy tends to endorse itself and imbecility, seldom an impediment to ambition, is often the spur, quickening the pace of aspiration. Goaded by ignorance, I imagined myself a wise man in the making, a savant in the manner of d'Alembert, Lalande, and the Marquis de Condorcet. I am accorded that honor now. The last living participant in the making of the meter, Jacques-François Darbon, is celebrated as the Sage of Tauzet, yet the only wisdom I know is that I am not a wise man. Marie-Jeanne and her goats taught me that lesson long ago.

A clever imbecile with a flair for mathematics, I had been removed from the military orphanage in Toulon when I was twelve and confided to the Oratoriens to be drilled in geometry, algebra, trigonometry, and, disappointingly, Catholic piety. Six years later, to the dismay of my religious instructors, who expressed a marked preference for the local penal colony, the college commended me to the *École des Ponts et Chaussées*, where I succumbed to a melancholy normally the preserve

of the privileged and studiously neglected my studies, dedicating myself instead to dissipation and a distracting passion for astronomy.

Even as a child, long before my mind had been
directed toward higher things, the night sky had been
a comfort in moments of disaffection, a promise of
something other, something beyond my immediate
sphere of being, a canvas on which I could stitch pictures nobody else saw. Adrift in the capital, at odds
with myself, and in need of celestial relief, I fell in
with a company of schoolmen prosperous enough to
purchase telescopic equipment, a rowdy gang of ram-
bunctious Gascons and incomprehensible Bretons,
with whom I spent many happy nights on the roofs of
Paris identifying comets and constellations, followed
by festive mornings roistering in the hostels beyond
the city gates, and less felicitous afternoons slumber-
ing over tavern tables. Exasperated at the ingratitude
of a parvenu plucked from obscurity by the generosity
of the *Ancien Regime,* the faculty duly expelled me. It
was the greatest gift my masters might have bestowed
on me.

At the time, though, the advantages of my demo-
tion were elusive to the point of invisibility. A young
man footloose in the most famous city in the world, a
young man familiar with the heavens and no stranger
to heavenly bodies on earth, a young man free to make
of himself what he might, I was yet at a loss as to
what to do with myself, more at a loss on earth than
in the stars, and it was only through the kindly intervention of one of my former professors that I found a
temporary appointment as tutor to a tax-farmer's son.

Teaching is the best way of learning, for the impart-
ing of knowledge implies its presence, in consequence
of which I rapidly acquired the rudiments of a more

patrician education, complementing with classical fancies the practical mathematics and modern languages I had studied previously. I also discovered that I was a capable draftsman, an aptitude that manifested itself in likeness sketches and topographical drawing, mapmaking proving almost as compelling as stargazing for one who had failed to place himself in the world.

Thus when the call went out for assistant geographical engineers to aid Messrs. Delambre and Mechain in remeasuring the Paris meridian, young Jacques-François had all the necessary skills: I was sound of limb (let the mind look to itself), as a child of the littoral I could swim (no self-respecting surveyor would let a mere river prevent him measuring an angle or taking flight from a hostile mob), my vernacular was the dialect of the south where the mountains were poorly mapped, I was acquainted with astronomy and the principles of geodesy, and I was unattached, therefore more readily dispensable than a married man. And I was an imbecile. Did I mention that? It was not the least of my attributes, not when recommending oneself for an adventure that was as perilous as it was ambitious.

—∿∿—

To be called Jacques-François on the eve of the rise to power of the Jacobin Club might be considered propitious for a young man yet to make his mark in the newly self-heeding nation of France, but I was never given to politics and derived no advantage from nominative happenstance. On the contrary, being *of* the nation brought me considerable troubles, as did my pretensions to being a savant.

I was, of course, familiar with the ferment of Paris. During my time as tutor, I had lived as high as my means allowed, carousing with the voluble pamphleteers, polemicists, and utopists who frequented the city's literary societies, so I knew the language of froth and fury that dampens temperance and kindles fanaticism. Yet to my mind the scientific project that ran parallel to the political turmoil was quite as momentous. Now that the meter has been accepted, it is difficult to understand just how radical this undertaking was.

Until the last century, this country was cluttered with a muddle of mismatched weights and measures that complicated trade and fostered confusion, a babel of kings' feet, tailors' elbows, carpenters' digits, and plumbers' thumbs; the Paris pint was not the provincial pint, a league in Picardy was longer than a league in Poitou, an ell of silk was shorter than an ell of linen, a baker's pound was lighter than an ironmonger's, fields were measured by labor or yield rather than surface area, definitions varied from village to village, and some measures were so flexible that nobody knew what they meant at all. The system was systematically unsystematic, a bane to honest men and a boon to bamboozling mountebanks.

The dream of rational men was to remedy this disorder by engineering a system in which all dimensions were coherent, uniform, and fixed, a system that did not favor one man over another, but which would facilitate trade, resolve food shortages, and nurture rationality in its users. In retrospect I can see a flaw here. The notion that people are rational, or might even wish to be so, is irrational in itself, but every age has its weakness, and ours was a faith in human reason.

The standard upon which the new measures were to be based was the earth itself. By remeasuring the meridian arc with modern instruments, we could compute the precise dimensions of the planet. The new base unit of length, upon which all other measurements would be premised, would be one ten-millionth of the distance from the North Pole to the Equator. Derived from nature, which is the patrimony of all mankind, the system would transform human relations, eradicating exploitation, subverting injustice, and uniting all people of all nations for all time. Persuading the public that this was a good idea was something else. As Rousseau said, *Men always prefer a worse way of knowing to a better way of learning.* But one should never underestimate the rational man's capacity for wild optimism, even when faced with something so intractable and unforgivable as human nature.

The technique for measuring an arc is triangulation. Selecting three elevated points within sight of one another, the surveyor projects a triangle onto the land. After measuring the angles at two of the viewing platforms and the distance between them, he can calculate how far the third point is from the first two. Adding a fourth visible elevation creates a second triangle, the dimensions of which can be determined by elementary trigonometry. Make a chain of triangles, take astronomical sightings to establish the latitude at either end, and the full quarter arc can be figured, from which we can deduce the size of the world.

But reforming mankind is a risky business. Most often mankind doesn't want to be reformed, not by a lot of bumptious Parisian academics, and surveyors had never been very popular. A traveler with nothing to sell was either a tax collector or a thief, which amounted to much the same thing in the eyes of the provincial peasantry. When he unpacked a lot of mysterious instruments he was a spy or a peddler of sinister weaponry. Once he started writing down weird symbols and consulting incomprehensible logarithmic tables, he was a wizard, responsible for sick cows, wayward wives, and poor harvests. Any man climbing a remote mountain just for the view must be up to no good and it served him right if he was waylaid by brigands. For some communities, the consternation caused by encountering a geographical engineer was altogether too much and the peasants would set upon the hapless surveyor with fists, farm implements, and anything hard that came to hand. And even the most forbearing farmer was inclined to set his dogs on you when you aimed a theodolite in his general direction. You really did need to be able to run away. It's always a useful talent, running away.

Yet I was a keen recruit. The project was an escape from the impasse I had created for myself, a call to adventure, and if I was running away, I was running away to danger. My job was to prepare the ground for Monsieur Mechain. Traveling south, I was to inspect old triangulation stations, search for a workable chain of triangles in the foothills of the Pyrenees, and conduct a preliminary survey of poorly mapped terrain near the village of Tauzet in the Fenouillèdes. It was this last task that excited me most.

My previous employer had possessed several sheets of the Academy map, which I used with my pupil to illustrate lessons in topography and history. The Cassini publication is a marvel of precision, but it does not identify dwellings, and we would amuse ourselves by copying maps of nearby hamlets then making excursions to fill in the lacunae. Sometimes, moved by mischief, we would even invent entirely fictional topographical details. There is a peculiarly puerile pleasure to be had from replacing a *seigneurial* manor with a midden. It was during these sorties that I discovered the fascinating challenge of mapping, the narrative spell of deciding what to include and what to exclude, what matters in the picture we want to draw as we represent a version of the world on paper.

A map is a way of reading the world. It doesn't describe what we see, it describes an idea of what we see, and what we value in what we see. It is a way of telling stories to ourselves, and from what I have observed, that is what most of us do most of the time, tell ourselves stories, about ourselves, our neighbors, our friends, our enemies, and our improbable spatchcocked planet. I had been given the opportunity to write my own map of the world. The story it told would become the map of my life.

I LEFT Paris in May. The month is fixed in my mind because afterward I would have no reliable news from the capital for upward of a year, living instead in a limbo of unknowing where nothing was certain, everything rumored. Even the stories of the king's flight and the Champ de Mars Massacre were garbled by the time they reached the provinces, hearsay inflamed by an atmosphere of suspicion and fear in which everyone might be a traitor to someone, and every report mistaken for the malicious propaganda of a foreign regime.

For many it would have been a living death to leave Paris, the polestar of power, money, and culture. For many who stayed, it would be a real death. For me, departure was deliverance, stepping into the unknown

like a true mapmaker venturing into uncharted terrain. I had been equipped with a theodolite (an antique
older than myself), an even more antediluvian quadrant, a circumferentor, a telescope, logarithmic tables,
a barometer, a military perambulator, a spirit level,
and an alidade scope for a plain table. Now that I
think about it, the apparatus was so superannuated
that I suspect they had a store cupboard they wanted
empty, but the instruments were adequate for the
purposes of my preliminary surveys. I was also provided with the relevant Cassini maps on a reduced
scale for locating triangulation stations, plus letters
of credit for disbursements where new platforms had
to be built, and a *laissez passer* in the king's name, a
passport that was to prove more hindrance than help
within the month.

Those first weeks on the road were uneventful.
With an advance on my salary, I had bought a Molly
mule for portage with a view to selling her at journey's
end, and for several days my energies were employed
overcoming her steadfast reluctance to stir her legs. I
suspect I'd saved her from the glue factory and for a
while it looked like the weight of my equipment would
render her just as swiftly. However, after a week we
reached an agreement, whereby she consented to
move provided she set the pace. The pace she chose
was so sedate that I was able to do much of my work
en route without stopping in each place overnight, as
I had time to visit belvederes and promontories while
the poor creature plodded on, enveloped in an air of
ineffable grief, her manner so doleful that even the
most desperate thief let her pass unmolested.

Despite the understanding between Molly and me,
the farther we got from Paris, the more we had to
stop. Many of the stations used in earlier surveys were

no longer functional. Wooden towers had been taken apart for the nails, castle keeps had collapsed, and belfries had been razed as symptomatic of a church that had got well above itself. Problems like these entailed tedious delays negotiating new stations, ordering repairs, and contracting artisans, delays made no easier by the fact that betimes I was bound to sleep on nothing better than bales of straw or a few planks haphazardly propped on a couple of trestles.

I also had to make time to prepare dispatches for my superiors in Paris. I spent many hours drafting these documents, though I never had a word back, despite having six courier posts en route where scientifically minded magistrates, mayors, and notaries who had been apprised of the project were supposed to receive correspondence from Paris. It was as if I was working in a void. I did not know then the delays and vicissitudes to which the project's principals were subjected. All I knew was that I was writing voluminous reports on my progress and nobody seemed to be reading them at all. With hindsight, I can understand why they might have chosen to ignore them. It was not merely that Messrs. Delambre and Mechain had problems of their own, but my outpourings were composed in a young man's prose, flamboyant and desperately unsure of itself. I'd be tempted not to reply to such flowery effusions myself now.

There were other incidental delays too. Given the facility with which I executed them, I had little esteem for my drawings, but in rural places the most rudimentary art was regarded as an act of uncommon prestidigitation. I only had to settle down with my sketchbook and I would soon be surrounded by a small crowd. People would huddle close, some tentatively touching the tip of my pencil to test its magic, and when the idea got about that a stick of graphite might reproduce anything, they would be demanding portraits of themselves. I also learned that it wasn't a good idea to show my maps, for once their purpose had been ascertained (a lengthy process in itself, people in the lowlands being mystified by the idea that one might make a two-dimensional representation of terrain), everyone wanted to know where they were and I could lose up to half a day locating each peasant's dwelling, as if they feared they might no longer exist if they weren't on the map. But mindful of the hostility my predecessors had encountered, I was glad they regarded the documents in a benign light. Then I came to the town of Vauriennes. The name still sends shivers down my spine.

⸺〰⸺

VAURIENNES IS a small place of which few will have heard, a neglect it richly deserves, but it lies on the meridian, so I was obliged to check its triangulation stations. Two of these remained viable, but the third, the steeple of the church, though still standing, was surrounded by such tall trees that the previous viewing point from the lantern apertures would no longer serve.

Leaving Molly tied to a trough in front of the church, I went to the presbytery. The priest's housekeeper was wary at first and nonplussed when I explained my purpose, but something in my manner must have suggested I was as inoffensive as I was unintelligible. Despite his grand title, Monsignor Larue was an unimposing man in a grubby purple gown speckled with so many minute burns that at first I thought somebody had left him out in the rain.

"I'm sorry," he said after I had explained the problem. "We can't cut the trees down. They shade the Sunday dances. The situation is delicate enough without me upsetting people. Would you care for one of these?" He offered me his tobacco pouch and a small square of paper cut from the *Gazette de France*. I rarely took tobacco at that time, but felt it would be undiplomatic to refuse. "I remember your predecessor," he said, lighting a taper at the fireplace, which in view of the season seemed to be maintained for this sole purpose.

"My predecessor?" I was slightly disturbed by this. I had supposed I was a herald of things to come rather than a memento of things past.

"Monsieur Deslongchamps. I was vicar at that time. He didn't like the trees either. But back then it was a just a question of distracting shadows. I never did see the maps they made. Here."

He held the taper to my scrappy cigarette, igniting an explosion of sparks that explained the state of his cassock.

"The Cassini survey, you mean? I can show you those maps."

Monsignor Larue disappeared behind his own small but lively Vesuvius.

"I would like to see them," he said, shaking the flame from the taper and patting out a spangling of incipient bonfires on his tummy. "And to discuss this project in more detail. In private, of course. The people here are greatly taken with recent events. They like nothing better than a pretext for disorder. But like many revolutionaries, they tend to conservatism in matters of consequence. Natural philosophy is considered a close cousin of necromancy."

"I am glad you see it in a different light," I said. "At least, I am supposing?"

"Contrary to popular opinion, ours is not the most regressive among the estates."

"You can see a solution then? To the trees."

"The trees stay. I wouldn't dare. But something can be arranged. The church is shingled. Perhaps if we were to make an opening in the spire. The added elevation might be sufficient."

I was quite taken aback. My previous experience of clerics had not been happy and I would never have expected a priest to propose knocking holes in church roofs. But when we went outside to inspect the spire, I discovered there were limits to what Monsignor Larue was prepared to do.

The first we knew that anything was amiss was the sound of a drum, shortly followed by the discordant piping of a flageolet and a trumpet. Molly had pricked up her ears and was looking about in a confused manner, though possibly she was troubled less by the noise itself than its provenance. I had noticed that she seemed hard of hearing. Whenever there was an unusual sound, she would glance suspiciously from side to side, aware that something was going on, but none too sure what or where it was coming from. In this instance, she did not have long to wait, for a most motley procession appeared at the corner of the square.

At its head, four sturdy lads sporting tricolor cockades shouldered the corners of a packing crate lid. Standing unsteadily on the lid was a crimson-cheeked young woman wearing a *bonnet rouge* and brandishing a pike, her dress pulled down at the bust to expose a bosom that would have brought tears of foreboding to a stay-maker. The palanquin was followed by what might loosely be described as the musicians, tooting, farting, and banging away, each oblivious to what the others were doing but giving it their best, apparently competing to promote their own (speaking loosely again) "tune" over that of their rivals. And behind them trailed what I sincerely hoped were the dregs of the town, because if they were anything else, Vauriennes was in serious trouble. Even in Paris, which likes to see itself as being in the vanguard of everything and has a rabble to match, I had rarely seen such an assortment of animated gargoyles. Several wielded jugs, sloshing wine onto the cobbles, and those who didn't showed every sign of having long since consumed the contents of their own jugs, possibly the jugs as well.

"Watch out, you fuckers! You nearly took my head off, you lousy blood rags."

The sturdy lads grinned delightedly, not in the least abashed by this tirade from their coy chatelaine, whose head they had clobbered on a milliner's blade sign.

"What on earth is that!" I said.

"I regret to say that is our young Rosalie," said Monsignor Larue, who was standing at my shoulder. "She works the Rue Soufflet. It is a family affair. At least three generations. I tried to redeem her mother, but she proved resistant to the promises of salvation."

Rosalie's litter bearers lurched to the right. Whether this was motivated by a desire to dance or simple crapulence I couldn't say, but the screeching it elicited from their charge would have made a fishwife blush. Curses rained down on the hapless porters, invoking all manner of anatomical havoc on their nether parts. Hoping to compensate, they lurched to the left, but this didn't remedy matters at all, and it was only due to a bit of deft work with her pike that Rosalie retained her footing, deft work that nearly took an eye out of poor Molly.

"I really think . . ." I said, turning to Monsignor Larue, but Monsignor Larue was no longer there. He had disappeared. Very wise too.

There was a patter of feet, a rush of air, a hiss of breath, and a screech that was blessedly free of lexical content. I faced the mob just in time to see Rosalie sailing toward me like a young bird turfed from its nest, a young bird encumbered by two improbably large breasts, a long gown, and a lot of liquor.

Noblesse oblige. As the pike shot overhead, I caught the young lady about the waist in a move that wouldn't have shamed a flat-handed wrestler. Unfortunately, Rosalie had gained such momentum that she won the bout and I ended up on my back, pinned down by her bubbies. In other circumstances, the situation might do, but right then it didn't do at all. One of Rosalie's acolytes was investigating Molly's packs and had come up with the quadrant. A blast of breath redolent of beer and onions caught me in the face.

"Hello," said Rosalie. "So what's a big boy like you doing in a place like this then?"

It was a question of some moment. Several other revelers had gathered about Molly and were delving into my baggage.

"My name's Marianne."

"What? I thought it was Rosalie. I say, please do leave those things alone."

"I'm the goddess of liberty."

That would explain the breasts then.

"They're really most valuable instruments." I was talking about the scientific equipment, though I don't doubt Rosalie's bosoms were of commensurate worth in her particular profession.

"Care to take a few liberties with me?"

"Yes, maybe some other time. Please, do excuse me. They're touching my tools."

"I know the feeling, my sausage, I know the feeling."

"Who are you? What's this?"

The speaker was an exceptionally loutish-looking individual, even by the standards of his confreres. He had a large, blotchy goiter that trembled when he spoke so that he resembled a toad giving voice to some tenebrous nocturnal caroling. Disentangling myself from Rosalie (no mean task in itself, for if I was a big boy, she was a very big girl), I hurried to recover my circumferentor, which the goiter was joggling in a most agitating manner. Another man was peering down the wrong end of the telescope with mounting puzzlement.

"Come, citizen, you have some explaining to do. What brings you here?"

This from a small, dark-complected individual who looked up at me slightly askance. Though less out-landish than his companions, his manner was more disquieting. He evidently held some sway over the others, because the jostling mob stilled, awaiting my response.

Thinking they might be cowed by the sheer audacity of the project, I told them: "I am part of an expedition sanctioned by the Assembly that intends to measure the world."

There was a moment's stunned silence, then, as one, they began howling with laughter. It was the funniest thing they had ever heard.

"What, all of it?"

"Bit big, isn't it?"

"Well, in its entirety, yes, of course. But we shall measure the meridian, then we can calculate the size of the earth."

"What's a meridian?"

"It's an imaginary line between two points on the earth's surface."

"An imaginary line?"

"Yes, that's right."

"And you want to measure it?"

This was even better. They fell about like I'd just lobbed a cannon ball in their midst.

"And where is it this imaginary line?"

"It can be anywhere you like really. It's arbitrary. It's just a measurable line on a curve."

"So's my pussy!"

"You tell him, Rosalie."

The lady in question had recovered herself and replaced her breasts inside her bodice. God knows how. There was enough tension there to snap the rivets on a chain-mail vest.

"Not imaginary, neither, her pussy isn't."

"You got an instrument for measuring that?"

"I've got an instrument I can lend him if he's paying."

"Too big for you, Didie. Rosalie would swallow you whole. You'd be needing one of them expeditions sanctioned by the Assembly."

I found all this most galling. These people were probably illiterate, yet they were presuming to mock matters that challenged some of the finest minds of the day . . . I mean measuring the world, not the dimensions of Rosalie's vulva. I wanted to ask them if they had read their *Mécanique Analytique* or the *Introduction à l'Analyse Infinitésimale*. Perhaps *La Résolution des Équations Numériques, Le Traité des Jonctions Analytique,* or the *Mémoire sur le Calcul des Probabilités?* To be honest, I hadn't read all these works myself, but at least I knew they existed. These people had all the intellectual rigor of a pair of slippers. I didn't like to tell them as much though. I doubted it would improve the situation.

"You still need to explain, citizen." It was my small dark friend, in no way distracted by the general hilarity. "You got that glass there. You might be a spy." It was then that I made my first mistake, for a mirthful mob is less menacing than a mistrustful mob, yet I contrived the transition from one state to the other almost effortlessly. I produced my *laissez passer,* anticipating that the document would be as intimidating as it was incomprehensible. The man could con his letters though and an ominous silence fell when he announced that I was the king's agent. "That would be Citizen Capet you're talking about, citizen. Your 'king,' I mean. He ran away, you know." It was the first I had heard of it. "That's treason, that is. You got a passport from a traitor. So, citizen, tell us, what are you doing here, carrying letters from a traitor?"

He was right, I really did need to explain. And I was ready for this. Or so I thought. Before leaving Paris, I had been instructed in my duties, instruction to which I had applied myself more assiduously than any previous study, for though I had courted rustication, it had severely shaken my confidence, and I felt compelled to prove myself the master of tasks for which I was, in truth, a mere apprentice. The melancholy that led to my expulsion from the school had been a curious thing, part dislocation, part arrogance, as if I were persuaded that, as a prodigy, I must perforce be a genius and above such humdrum pursuits

as study. The discovery that not everyone was overwhelmed by my brilliance was unnerving, leaving me
as intellectually insecure as I was intellectually able.
Yet I was unaware of this at the time. Folly is like
being dead, painless for the subject, who is ignorant
of his condition, but distressing for those nearby.
What ensued certainly proved painful for the people
in my immediate vicinity.

"Citizen?"

Since my instruments had inspired the crowd's
initial suspicions, I resolved to explain their purpose.
A shallow flight of steps led to the church portico.
Shouldering Molly's panniers, I climbed to the top
step and turned to address my audience.

"Now this telescope," I said, persuaded I might
clarify matters as lucidly as the optical instrument.
"It's nothing sinister. We simply use this for checking
sightlines. We need to be able to see clearly, after all,
if we are to work out where we are. And this perambulator is for measuring distances by counting how
many times the wheel turns between two points. These
other instruments are angle-measuring devices, so
that we can calculate positions, lengths, and heights.
I might use these, for example, to locate the church
or determine how tall the steeple is. And the barometer, that's this thing here, tells us how high we are
by measuring atmospheric pressure, as the weight of
air decreases the higher we go. So, you see, it's really
all very straightforward."

If my previous pronouncements had been greeted
as some of the tidiest witticisms of recent times, this
brief exposition oppressed my listeners like an opiate
without the euphoric qualities.

"What did he say?"

"He wants to know where he is."

"He doesn't know where he is? Isn't he here?"

"I think he's looking for the church."

"The big fool, it's behind him."

"The weight of air? Air's not heavy!"

"No, it's how high he is. That's what he wants to know."

"I can tell him how high he is without any fancy instruments."

One of Rosalie's porters had procured a length of rope. Not good. Not good, at all.

"But this is all perfectly innocent," I protested. "Our purpose is simply to liberate ordinary men and women from dependence on better educated people."

"People like you, citizen?"

It's always imprudent to imply you are superior to other people, particularly when they've got a rope in their hands, but the didactic impulse overpowered me. I described, in harrowing detail, how the meridian project would work, how it would improve life for everybody, how wonderful it all was, but judging by the glazed look in my listeners' eyes, I would have been better off resorting to a more expeditious solution, like Monsignor Larue, and employing shanks' pony. I was already learning a lively appreciation of reason's limitations.

"But why does he want to know how high he is?" Goiter-man was obsessing over this unfortunate detail. It was best to get this business of elevation settled before I was hoisted into another realm altogether.

"We wish to measure a straight line on the earth's surface. Only the earth is not flat, is it?"

"This bit's flat," he said.

"Yes, but taken as a whole, it's not flat, is it?"

"It's flat here and you want to measure it here."

I was beginning to feel a certain sympathy with my religious instructors' attempts to drill me in my catechism.

"Come on, Arnaud," said one of the other men, "you know the world's round."

Arnaud stroked his goiter.

"Is it?" he asked.

"More or less," I said, injudiciously. "There is some debate as to whether it is prolate or oblate. Men of science believe the earth is not a perfect sphere, like an orange say, but might be pointy at each pole, like a lemon, or a bit flat at the top and bottom, like a . . . like an apple or perhaps a lentil."

"What's he saying now?"

"He's saying the world is oranges and lemons and apples and lentils."

"He's a loony. Let's kill him."

"Look, no, please, listen. We're getting off the subject here."

"No, we're not, hang him!"

We were though. The controversy about the shape of the earth was only really of interest to mapmakers and mariners, as it would distort the length of a degree of longitude in relation to the equator. Thankfully, I hadn't told them that, according to Lacaille's calculations, the world was pear shaped. I don't think they could have coped with that.

"Please, listen! I am trying to explain the complexity of measuring a long line on the earth's surface. The angles of a triangle on a curve don't equal 180 degrees. So we have to correct for this. And to accurately compute the meridian, we must adjust measured distances to sea level, so we need to know the heights of observation points. Accuracy is essential if we are to achieve perfection and that is what we seek, the better to serve science and mankind as a whole. The world is an uncooperative place and natural philosophers must compensate for its eccentricities. By rectifying the distortions of reality, we make it conform to the more harmonious tenets of theory."

I felt I had carried this off rather well, not without a certain pedagogical restraint, resisting the temptation to overload my listeners with the intricacies of vertices and refraction. But words have a way of transporting us into places not entirely consistent with actuality and my appraisal of the performance was not widely shared.

"I've had enough of this."

A noose had been fashioned in the rope. Arnaud grabbed me, his goiter wobbling alarmingly, and dragged me down the stairs. Rough hands seized me from either side. No longer the focus of attention, Rosalie was sitting on the edge of the trough, exploring her left nostril with her pinkie. This would be my last sight on earth, a bored prostitute picking her nose.

There was a clattering of hooves and half a dozen horsemen rattled into the square from behind the church. At their head, was a short, pudgy man wearing a sash in the same colors as the cockades of Rosalie's porters. He reined in his horse and pointed at me in a furious manner that suggested his finger might be a gun.

"This man is under arrest!"

—⁓—

MONSIGNOR LARUE examined my maps. I have one still, dotted with tiny burns, long since faded from black to brown.

"I apologize for my pusillanimity," he said, handing me his tobacco pouch. "But I have learned that it is best to absent myself in these moments of revolutionary zeal. I had not thought they would trouble you."

"You saved me by fetching the mayor," I said. "And no harm was done to my instruments. Only to my pride. But I did not think those ruffians would let me go so easily."

"You should never underestimate the Frenchman's respect for authority," he said, licking the paper to seal a cigarette. "Even in times such as these. The ordinary man may be inclined to overturn the old order, but only the better to obey the new. Sadly our freethinking writers have done such a thorough job vilifying the church that we maintain no credit with the people and cannot expect our former authority to be respected in the same way."

"It was my hope that reason might sway them."

"You had reason, they had rancor. The parties were not equal. You should take the mayor's advice, you know. Move on tomorrow. We will see to your platform. It is interesting, this business of the meridian." Monsignor Larue lit his cigarette and a spattering of new landmarks landed on the map. "You know the church sanctioned a similar project? Father Boscovich was calculating the length of a degree on the Italian meridian when he died a few years ago."

"I am surprised the Pope approved of such work."

"I'm not sure His Holiness approved. But he knows the church cannot ignore the science for long. We need people who understand it on our side. And besides, measurement ought to be a matter for the church. It is a product of The Fall, after all."

"I had thought it more a manifestation of civilization," I said. "Counting things. It's one of the criteria, isn't it? Like agriculture, writing, clothing, viticulture."

Though the wine he had served was no token of civilization. It was thin, vinegary stuff from a poorly bunged barrel. The dark tobacco helped mitigate the astringency.

"The two statements are not contradictory," he said. "*By the sweat of thy brow shalt thou eat bread.* You should study your bible better. We work because we have been expelled from Eden. Ask a peasant, he'll tell you all about civilization. We dress ourselves and get drunk for much the same reason. And writing may well be nothing more than a desperate attempt to recover a lost paradise. As for numbers, they are definitely the devil's playthings. *Satan stood up against Israel and provoked David to number Israel.* It is the only time Satan is a named entity in the Old Testament, as if the census were truly diabolic. We count things because we can no longer trust our fellow men. Your universal measure is a symptom of mankind's duplicity."

I learned later that Monsignor Larue was drowned during the September Massacres, which saddened me greatly. He was an erudite man, his only apparent vice an addiction to tobacco. Like many young men in those days, I was not merely irreligious but actively anticlerical. I had always been troubled by people who said they talked to an invisible being who governed the world. More worrying still was when they claimed the invisible being talked back to them and told them what to do. My best hope was that they were listening to themselves and were otherwise sensible individuals. But the murder of Monsignor Larue made me realize that there is an even more questionable category of person, those who hate the ones talking to invisible beings so much that they feel such people shouldn't be talking to anybody ever again. You know the world has gone awry when people with fantasy friends get killed for it.

And there was wisdom in what Monsignor Larue said about writing and paradise. Nearly every creative work craves a lost Arcadia, even when the ideal is one we have never known. Like an antiquarian reconstructing a pitcher from shards of pottery, fabricators of all kinds aim to re-create the world from fragments of reality, trying to piece together a perfect shape dimly glimpsed elsewhere. But whatever men make will always be cracked. Perfection doesn't exist. The earth itself is not a perfect sphere. It's not even symmetrical. And it moves in most mysterious ways. Our world is warped and we are bent out of shape. The belief that things can be otherwise is the greatest illusion of rational utopias.

My DISPATCH about Vauriennes was unusually febrile, even by my standards, but in the coming days, I discovered repeatedly how precarious the life of a geographical engineer can be. I was a master of disaster, adept at eliciting catastrophe yet deftly evading calamitous consequences, albeit as much by luck as cunning.

On a chill morning near Salers, I fell off a farm chimney where I hoped to raise a platform and only escaped serious injury because I landed in a muddy pigsty. The pig wasn't pleased. Neither was the farmer's wife, whom I prevailed upon to clean my clothes, while I huddled under a blanket beside a bubbling cauldron of gruel. Investigating a campanile north of

Rodez, I was accused of being a bell thief, an alle-
gation so bizarre that I was at a loss to respond. It
was only when the bell tower master saw Molly that
he conceded even the most inept malefactor wouldn't
abscond with purloined bells on such a decrepit
nag. Farther south, I was warned against entering
an abandoned abbey because it was haunted by the
ghosts of malevolent monks. After narrowly avoiding
being turned into a ghost myself by falling masonry, I
decided it would be wiser to ask the local magistrate
to arrange for a wooden tower to be built alongside the
ruin. On another occasion, I got carpenters to raise
a scaffold on top of a stone obelisk commemorating
Cassini's 1740 survey, only to find it dismantled the
next morning. Apparently the platform was part of an
obscure counterrevolutionary plot. Given the prevail-
ing atmosphere of mistrust and hovering violence, I
did not inquire into the particulars of the supposed
plot and simply filed a report to the effect that a new
station would require armed guards.

The most frightening of these misadventures was
also the most farcical. We were traversing a forest of
chestnut trees near Saint Pons when a shabby figure
plunged from the undergrowth. Molly didn't take
kindly to this, being no less keen on sudden movements than unexpected noises, which may have been
germane to the outcome of the encounter. She jerked
back on her halter and it took me a moment to calm
her, by which time the man was beside us. He was
standing on the other side of Molly. I didn't need to
ask what he wanted. The pistol leveled across the
mule's back spoke volumes. I knew nothing of guns
and, though I've had cause to use them since, pride
myself on knowing little enough now. But even an

imbecile understands that having a pistol pointed at you is not a good thing. Molly didn't think so either.

She hadn't exactly been docile in the early days, but she had been placid, her principal preoccupations being drink, food, and rest (a very respectable philosophy of life), so I was as unprepared as our assailant for what happened next. The stock of the gun grazed the base of Molly's withers. Her response was instantaneous. She whirled round and bit him, hard. I don't imagine he did much sitting for the next few weeks. The pistol went off with a deafening blast, the ball tearing into the trees behind me. Molly ripped the rope from my grip and galloped down the track like she was nearing the finishing line at the Fontainebleau hippodrome. The highwayman was so surprised that he didn't even howl with pain. He just stood there gaping. I grabbed his gun, hurled it into the thicket, and dashed after Molly. The sudden turn of speed very nearly killed her. We had to lay over two days at the next town for her to recover. But it was an instructive lesson. When it comes to armed combat, a mule is a better weapon than a gun. I was becoming rather fond of Molly and wondered whether I would sell her at journey's end after all.

For all my mishaps, there was still something deeply satisfying about tracking the meridian arc, stalking a straight line only the scientific mind could detect rather than restricting myself to the vagaries of rivers and roads that any fool could follow. Nature can be so wayward, man-made routes no less so, but a purely cerebral construct aspires to a kind of purity beyond its practical applications. And on the occasions when I had to build a new tower, there was the thrill of seeing views nobody had seen before, standing high above the land conjuring it into being. It was as if I was inventing the notion and nation of France, giving birth to an abstraction. You will forgive a young man's hubris evident in these conceits, but in this memoir I aim to be as true to the person I was as to the person I have become, and in those days I valued straight lines and lofty perspectives above the crooked ways and secluded corners I have since learned to love.

———

Half a dozen goats were dotted about the cliff face, standing nonchalantly on nothing very evident, their purchase as improbable as the clumps of shrubs that clung to scraps of soil in the cracked rock. From the track below, the mountain looked sheer, an optical illusion that did nothing to detract from the apparent impossibility of the goats' perches.

A girl appeared at the top of the cliff. She was wearing a light tunic, little more than a petticoat, the hem fluttering in the heat like a lazily flapping flag. The skirts covered the knees but the sleeves were cut short leaving her arms exposed to the sun. Her hair was wrapped in a cloth tied at the nape of her neck like a bohemian. She had a large bale of firewood strapped to her back. She paused a moment, looking down at me, then stepped off the edge of the cliff.

She wouldn't have heard, but I gasped aloud, a strangled cry of warning, for she must surely fall to her death. But instead of plunging to the ground, she nimbly skipped across the face of the mountain, her clogs clacking on indiscernible ledges etched in the granite. She moved with appalling insouciance, as if the descent was no more dramatic than a country dance.

The girl whistled and the goats headed toward her, their movements choreographed in a vertical ballet, zigzagging back and forth across the cliff, occasionally kicking free whispers of scree that tumbled down taking my heart with them. Closing toward a declivity at the base of the cliff, the company touched earth a few strides from where I was standing, clutching Molly's halter, as if holding her tight might safeguard the cliff-face acrobats.

My heart continued to tumble, for though the girl was no classical beauty, her weathered complexion alone precluded that, everything about her was agreeable to the eye. She had a well-shaped head (the cranium very round under the tightly wrapped scarf), a broad brow, wide-set eyes, and a full mouth defined by strong laugh lines and high cheekbones. She looked forthright and unflinching, and was physically strong, too, for the firewood must have weighed as much as one of her goats, yet she carried it like a bouquet of herbs. The only signs of strain were a fine sheen of perspiration on her upper lip and a single small vein pulsing in the muscle of each upper arm, dark blue against the brown skin. She was close enough for me to catch a pleasant scent of woodsmoke and rosemary behind the gamy aroma of the goats.

"I'm looking for Tauzet," I said.

The eyes were very dark, almost black in the bright light, and creased at the corners.

"You've found her," she said, as if claiming *she* was the place I was looking for. The lips stiffened slightly, stifling a smile. She nodded at the mountain behind her. "The Pech de Tauzet."

"Oh, I see. No, I mean the village. I need a room."

I could imagine waking up to those dark eyes and that amused mouth.

"Follow me," she said.

I followed. Believe me, I followed. Molly too. And the goats. We were all smitten.

—⁓—

THERE WAS nothing in this, not on my part, at least. I couldn't speak for Molly and the goats. Maybe they knew better. But for me it was just a young man's fancy. There is a stage in life when gawking at girls is as compelling as it is inconsequential. I remember times when I could fall in love with half a dozen different women a day, all of whom have long since faded from memory. It is simply the way of young men, especially the dimmer sort. When we met, Marie-Jeanne was just one more woman in a world full of women who made my heart flip, and as I followed her into the village, I had no idea that I was embarking on a romantic adventure that would change my life. Nonetheless, I won't pretend I wasn't glad when, my inquiries in Tauzet receiving negative responses, her father offered me lodging. I could think of worse company.

The Cazalets lived in a cottage beside one of Berenguer's sheepfolds. They had a house in the village too. Berenguer was a wealthy man by local standards, but preferred living at one remove, which suited me. My presence was bound to excite suspicion and it was best to be away from prying eyes. Already my initial request for accommodation had been greeted sourly by the man designated communal factor for the year, a surly individual with a wall-eye that was always looking elsewhere, as if he suspected something more interesting might be happening next door. The mayor was equally disobliging and the priest was a poor creature prone to peevish spluttering, giving the impression that his interlocutor was being willfully exasperating. Within the week it was rumored that I had been sent by the authorities to pursue smugglers, that I was a government agent intent on raising the *taille* (despite the fact that the tax had been abolished), and that I was a mining engineer prospecting for silver. It was preferable if my comings and goings were witnessed as little as possible. After Vauriennes, I was wary of explanations.

Old man Cazalet was a widower, his wife having died giving birth to Marie-Jeanne's brother, Ramond, about whom father and daughter were unforthcoming, saying only that he was with his father's flocks in the summer pasture. Berenguer was an easygoing man, content to spend his days sitting on a rush chair in the shade of the sheepfold, sipping *clairet*, reading old almanacs and tattered chapbooks from the *Bibliotèque Bleue.* His daughter saw to the household, cooked over an open hearth, and tended the goats that kept them in milk and cheese during the summer while the sheep were in the high mountains.

Marie-Jeanne was given great latitude by her father. I never heard him forbid her anything and had the impression she had been at liberty from a young age. He was startled on the second night when I sought his permission for her to help me with my work. I had been explaining (as approximately as I dared, I didn't want another young woman mocking me like Rosalie) the purpose and practice of my mission. The first task of any survey is to walk the land and Marie-Jeanne had offered to guide me.

"My daughter does as she pleases," said Berenguer after I'd asked if he minded her accompanying me. His words were in no way reproachful, simply a statement of something that ought to have been obvious to all but an imbecile. He didn't know who he was dealing with.

"I thought perhaps she might be missed about the farm," I said.

"She is not busy," said Marie-Jeanne, eyeing me coolly. "While the sheep are in the mountains, she has little to do. And like her father says, she does as she pleases. And she must take the goats out anyway. And she wagers the goats walk as well as Monsieur."

Berenguer bit his lip and turned aside with a small smile.

"Of course, if she will do," she added.

I accepted the reproof.

"She will do very well," I said.

———

My CONTRIBUTION to the development of topographical drawing is slim. The Map of Love and my Murder Map might seem original, but they were no more than temporal versions of those medieval maps when cartographers concocted whimsical visions of the world designed to evoke a spiritual response. However, I am reasonably certain that no other surveyor ever went to work with a herd of ruminants, which is a pity, because Marie-Jeanne's animals were affable creatures, and I have since participated in expeditions on which I would have gladly swapped my companions for a couple of goats. Footpaths rarely go where surveyors want to go, but I never yet met a goat that moaned about rough ground, and on occasion their inveterate inquisitiveness can find ways up places that are manifestly impassable from below.

While Molly applied herself to Berenguer's stock of hay, Marie-Jeanne and I went exploring. I needed to make a map of the area around Tauzet and identify potential triangulation stations. That first morning we toured the entire commune so that I might get an overall impression of the landscape. It was as well I had walked so far in the preceding weeks, for otherwise I would not have been able to keep up with my guide, who capered about the hills as if they were pudding-sized hummocks.

Happily, she did not take me up the cliff face I had seen her descending when I arrived, but we did approach the *pech* from a different direction, pausing near the top to eat the provisions she had brought: goat cheese, flat bread, black olives, and a flask of Berenguer's wine, a meal that would become a ritual on our excursions. When the food was finished, I opened my satchel to get out the *Carte de Roussel* for the region, a military map made a lifetime earlier, but the best we had for the Pyrenean foothills. Marie-Jeanne leaned close giving me the opportunity to breathe in that beguiling scent of woodsmoke and rosemary.

"He's spelled it wrong," she said. "There, Tauzet, it's 'z - e - t' at the end, not 'x - e.'"

"You can read?"

"Of course I can. My father taught me. And that mountain, that's not over there. Look."

She was right. Roussel had conjured a hill to the west where none existed at all.

"Have you ever seen a map before?"

"A woodcut in a gazette once," she said, still scanning the map, oblivious to my incredulity. "But not a real map, no."

"Yet you can understand this?"

"I spend all my time up high looking down. And look, he hasn't named the *Saut de Procureur*. That's where we are here, this cliff."

I was nonplussed. Most people seeing a map for the first time ask *Where are we?* That's why maps exist, to answer that question. You're not meant to place yourself so unerringly. It seemed almost blasphemous. You don't want the uninitiated understanding things before you've even told them what they don't know. Though you never could outwit Marie-Jeanne. I couldn't, at least. I once told her I wanted to be a savant. She asked what that was. I told her it was someone who knew things. Then we are all savants, she said, which wasn't what I meant at all. She has an unsettling way of looking round corners, as if the walls aren't there at all.

"The *Saut de Procureur*, what a peculiar name," I said, to cover my confusion. "Are you telling me a public prosecutor came here to kill himself?"

"I'm not sure he killed himself. I think the jumping was done for him. Government men aren't well liked in Tauzet. If one of them has a little accident, it's no crime."

At which point one of the goats peered over my shoulder. Puckering her lips, she gently burped in my face.

"She likes you," said Marie-Jeanne.

Being patronized by a goat was a novel experience. I considered pointing out that I was a geographical engineer employed on an extremely complicated scientific expedition of the utmost importance with far reaching consequences for the well-being of humanity, but decided against it. Similar sentiments hadn't gone down well in Vauriennes.

"I'm glad to hear it," I said. "Apparently not being liked round here can prove fatal."

We spent the rest of that afternoon poring over the map, Marie-Jeanne pointing out its failings and naming places that were accurately represented. She had a remarkable eye for detail, so much so that I resolved to make a plain table and begin mapping straight away. The business of identifying workable triangulation stations could wait till I was more familiar with the terrain.

———✺———

A week later, the first map sheet was nearly complete. The first day I had constructed the table, closely watched by Marie-Jeanne while her goats, left to their own devices, stripped bark from the baseboards on the barn wall. Berenguer had provided timber for the table top. Six splints of mortised planks with dowel pins served as an adjustable tripod. Once I had installed the spirit level and alidade, I was able to proceed with my drawing.

I tested the system on the outskirts of the village, which probably wasn't a good idea. We were seen by a couple of basket weavers who regarded my drawing with an air of baleful mistrust, hurrying on before I could commit some pernicious act of diabolic sorcery. Marie-Jeanne, however, was fascinated by the technique and watched the work so closely that the goats, having acquired a taste for a good bit of bark, invaded an outlying orchard, providing a charming pastoral spectacle that Marie-Antoinette might have appreciated in the Petit Trianon but which wasn't at all popular with the local peasants.

For the actual survey, we set ourselves up on the *pech*, that being the highest elevation in the vicinity. Marie-Jeanne continued to scrutinize my work, questioning me on what I was doing and why. She was so engrossed by the process that I thought I might show her how to use the table herself. The first consequence of this was that the *Saut de Procureur* nearly became the Surveyor's Plunge for I was so astonished by how quickly Marie-Jeanne picked up the technique of sighting and plotting points on the paper that I stepped back and almost toppled off the edge.

After measuring a baseline with the perambulator, I risked initiating her in the task of triangulation, both for measuring distances and calculating altitudes. It was a risk because I was still loath to expose myself to the incomprehension and ridicule talk of triangulation had inspired in the past. It was also a risk because, no matter how instinctive her grasp of topography, the necessary trigonometry needs must be totally alien to her. Yet she displayed an intuitive intelligence that would have been the envy of many scholars, manipulating the theodolite as skillfully and efficaciously as she milked a goat's udder, and even proving herself competent at computing despite never having done the work in the past. Her aptitude was such that the map progressed far more rapidly than had I been working on my own.

Being tied to the plain table entailed less walking, but we still covered a lot of ground, since problems of variable refraction meant we had to confirm altitude calculations using the barometer. It was during these peregrinations that our relationship developed as we walked and talked our world into being, she naming places we passed while I quizzed her about the village and the life they lived in this intermediate realm between the lowlands and the high country. She remained reticent when the talk turned to the whereabouts of Ramond, but responded to questions about herself openly.

"It's not easy living in a village like Tauzet," she said when I asked about the Cazalets' isolation, for nobody ever seemed to visit.

"You mean the hardships of the climate?"

"It comes from that. Surviving here, you have to rely on others. It's always been that way. And it shapes how people think. Individuals don't count. Only the community matters. To hold the village together, everybody has to behave the same way, do the same things, live the same lives. My father was always different. Too different. The reading alone set him apart. Most see it as wasting time. Even the teacher in the little school told him I read too much and he ought to knock it out of me. After mother died, well, you have seen how he is with me. I do as I please. People don't approve. Then there are the accidents of history."

"Accidents?"

"When I was fifteen, my father was appointed to collect the *taille*."

"He didn't do the job well?"

"A little too well. It just strengthened the feeling that we weren't really a part of the village. That's when we moved out to the cottage."

"You were forced out?"

"No, but life is easier like this. For us and for others."

I was expecting more, she had used the plural, but I didn't press her on the other "accidents." The Cazalets' solitude helped explain their willingness to take in a stranger, but it was an invitation that could only reinforce their isolation.

"People are not very understanding," I said.

"You have experience of it?" she asked.

I don't know why, but I started telling her about my mishap in Vauriennes. It was only when I reached the point in the narrative at which Rosalie had been pitched from her platform and was winging her way toward me that a snort alerted me to the fact that Marie-Jeanne found the episode funny. At first I was a little put out. No wonder she was shunned by the neighbors if she carried on like this. But then I felt a queer glow of satisfaction. It was agreeable to make a young girl laugh and she laughed well, wide open and deep down, not like the narrow snickering of people too cultivated to let themselves go. I liked the large sound she made. Warming to the task, I worked up the more farcical aspects of the encounter. I had thought to avoid being laughed at, but it didn't hurt, and it put the whole story in a different light.

"People are absurd," she said when I had finished.

I was none too sure whether she meant them or me, but I didn't much mind either way.

"Then we must be connoisseurs of human absurdity," I said, slightly startled at the idea, which hardly conformed to the spirit of rationality that motivated the mission I was involved in. Indeed, it was contrary to all the education I had received since leaving the orphanage. But already I was no longer quite the man I had been. Only ten days after my arrival, I could discern a certain sublimity in the daunting landscape to the south, the chaotic mountains that were by rights an affront to the rational desire for order.

"In present times, it is our best hope," she said.

Her words and a troop of horsemen galloping by in the distance were a salutary reminder of the state of

France. Men on horses never mean anyone any good
in my experience.

—◠◠◠—

THE WORST of the revolutionary tumult was no more
than hearsay in Tauzet, but the rumors were dramatic
enough. It was said that corporations had been abolished, that priests were forbidden their vestments,
that martial law had been declared, that parliament
was urging citizens to disobey the government, that
prisoners were being massacred, that Prussian armies
were massing on the border, and I don't know what
else. It was all so improbable that I wouldn't have
been surprised to hear the Pope had married "Citizen
Capet" and the happy couple were last seen waltz-
ing off into the sunset to celebrate their nuptials with
the king of Sweden. I exaggerate, but only a little, for
once you get a taste for human absurdity, anything
seems possible. Nobody knew if these reports were
true or merely the invention of some fevered imagination down the road, but when the world is upended,
everything is as credible as it is incredible. It was only
much later that I discovered all these things had actually happened. Except, of course, for the bit about the
Pope's wedding.

Yet even out on the edges, disorder and danger
were never far away. The horsemen we had seen were
probably one of the militias that were being set up
even in the remotest villages, groups dispensing revolutionary justice as they saw fit, the definition often
as not governed by local rivalries and resentments.
It was striking how many people we did see abroad.
Many villagers were absent, the shepherds in the
mountains, day laborers harvesting in Spain and on

the coastal plains, but for all the savage emptiness of the hinterland, we were never entirely alone, and most encounters had to be treated with caution.

Several times we saw smugglers' mule trains, going about their business quite openly, but it was as well to make yourself scarce when they were around, for there was no knowing how they would react to a "government man" like me. Likewise the local *bandoliers*, who could be civil enough when they wanted, but remained professional robbers for all that. It was even said that Spanish *miquelets*, partisans who diverted themselves between wars with a little light banditry, were emboldened by the chaos in France and venturing across the border, doubtless passing the smugglers going the other way.

To avoid being seen by the horsemen, Marie-Jeanne and I climbed a small wooded hill in the lee of the Pech de Tauzet. The slope was stippled with rocks that stood clear of the stunted trees. We had taken sightings on these outcrops to estimate the gradient and now used one as shelter, settling down on the near side of a stack, where we thought, mistakenly as it turned out, nobody would see us. Marie-Jeanne had been carrying the table top with the map pinned to it and she now began to inspect our handiwork.

Any student of history will know that any invention of any consequence is invariably claimed by every civilized country in the world, a competition that is particularly intense between close rivals like France and England. It is a practical and relatively painless way of irritating each other without the fuss of going to war. A French historian of mapping will tell you that contour lines were invented by the military engineer Jean-Baptiste Marie Charles Meusnier de la Place. The English will tell you it was the naturalist

Charles Hutton. Obviously, with such an august name as Jean-Baptiste Marie Charles Meusnier de la Place to hang on the discovery, the French have the more convincing claim (we're always better at sophisticating things with elaborate verbiage), but like all stories, history is personal, and for me the invention was Marie-Jeanne's.

"Why don't we draw a line between these dots," she said, pointing at the altitude points corresponding to the outcrops of rock.

"Why would we?" I asked.

"Because they're all at the same height," she said. "If you join up measurements on the same level, then do the same thing lower down and higher up, and do it all around the hill, you'll see the shape of the place and how steep it is."

It was as well I was already sitting down, otherwise the idea would have knocked me flat. I had been using conventional hachure lines to indicate the steepness and aspect of slopes, but these were impressionistic. What she was proposing was at once more precise, more elegant, and more informative, something that even an untrained eye could comprehend but which would incorporate accurate scientific recordings.

I didn't see the full potential of her suggestion at the time, but I was sufficiently moved to mention something that had been in my mind for some days. I had seen how excited people were by my sketches. I knew how intrigued Marie-Jeanne was by the practice of drawing. So to express my gratitude and admiration, I offered to do her portrait.

She responded to the idea with such artless enthusiasm that I resolved to make good my promise immediately. My sketchbook was in my satchel, we had done enough work for the day, so I positioned her on a patch of sward slightly above me and settled on a rock that allowed me to rest the sketchbook on my knees.

Rereading the above, the motives I outline are disingenuous. The truth is I liked watching Marie-Jeanne and wanted to draw her for my own sake. Drawing a portrait is a curiously intimate act. I don't mean in the normal ways, like kissing or making love, where the mingling of bodies makes the self less distinct. It's closer to cutting someone's hair, concentrating on each detail then standing back to look at the result and see if your touch is sure. And the looking is the thing. It is a pretext for observing someone with a closeness that would be intrusive, even offensive in nearly every other circumstance. Being looked at is sufficiently burdensome that you can almost sympathize with the plight of the Bourbons, who were under constant scrutiny from the morning bowel movement to their ceremonial disrobing at bedtime.

The work was particularly gratifying with Marie-Jeanne, for she was a good subject, brimming with pleasure, breathing deeply, her cheeks flushed, her whole being quivering with a fullness of life, but untouched by the stilted self-consciousness that affects many sitters. There was so much light inside her that she was almost illustrating herself. All I had to do was pay attention and point the pencil in the right direction. Attentiveness is vital to a good portrait. It's the foundation for virtually everything of value in life, reaching out, stretching oneself toward the disparate experiences and perceptions represented by other people and other lives. Drawing Marie-Jeanne, I was drawing myself into her, becoming her as I mapped the contours of her personality through the relief of her physical features.

I had nearly done when a shadow fell on the page. I had been so absorbed by my task that I hadn't heard the factor approaching. He was glaring at the portrait, at least as much as you can glare when one eye is wandering off in a different direction, but even the vagrant eye was angry.

"What's that?" he asked.

"It's mine," said Marie-Jeanne, jumping up to snatch the sketchbook as if she feared he might steal it. I was pleased to see something soften in her eye when she looked at the likeness.

"It's just a portrait," I said.

"She's having her portrait done now, is she?"

I didn't bother replying as the basic fact was evident, but I suspected something else was implied by the remark.

"We're setting up a revolutionary committee in the village," he said.

"Congratulations," I said. "And what exactly is a revolutionary committee?"

The comment was malicious, but I had no reason to love the man and Marie-Jeanne's sentiments toward him were clearly even less warm. He hesitated.

"It's a committee," he said. "For the revolution."

"Oh, well done."

Marie-Jeanne laughed. The stray eye did a little dance of pique. Provoking him was foolish, but I had a feeling I was ready for far greater folly if it made her laugh.

"Meeting tomorrow morning. In the church at the third hour. You are summoned to appear before the committee. To explain yourself."

That was ambitious. I barely knew myself. The idea that I might explain myself to others, let alone something so nebulous as a revolutionary committee, was fanciful in the extreme.

"And bring those . . . those things you're doing."

"The map?"

"Whatever."

In times of revolution, discretion is not always enough.

—~~—

THE COMMITTEE looked more like a tribunal. The mayor, the priest, and the factor were sitting on rush chairs behind a long table in front of the altar. They directed me to a wooden stool below the chancel. The rest of the villagers were crammed onto benches in the nave. Berenguer and Marie-Jeanne, whom I had tried to persuade not to come, stood at the back.

During the preliminaries, I expressed some surprise that Monsieur Le Curé was part of a revolutionary committee, inspiring a cascade of invective in which Monsieur Le Curé let it be known that if the Abbé de Périgord could be a deputy in the Assembly, there was no good reason why Monsieur Le Curé could not preside over a revolutionary committee, and he would thank Citizen Darbon to address him as Citizen Gabadou in all future exchanges. I discovered later that Citizen Gabadou was more flexible than Talleyrand himself when it came to convictions, capable of flitting between Citizen Gabadou and Monsieur Le Curé with rare facility as circumstances required. At the time, however, Citizen Darbon concluded it would be politic to accede to Citizen Gabadou's request, as Citizen Gabadou appeared to be sitting in judgment on Citizen Darbon. Anxious to get the nomenclature right, I turned to the factor.

"My apologies, but if I recall correctly, you are Citizen Dalbaret?"

The factor's wall-eye inspected the south transept, neither confirming nor denying his identity. According to Marie-Jeanne, Dalbaret had fought long and hard to avoid being appointed factor, and was so furious at his failure that he had resolved to exact every revenge on those who had brought about this unwanted elevation, to wit the rest of the world. I could not hope for much charity from that quarter.

"And you, citizen?"

My manner was a bit too jaunty for the mayor who, despite being perfectly bald, contrived to look as ruffled as his colleagues.

"Pellaprat," he said, curtly. "My name is Citizen Pellaprat."

Unlike the reluctant factor, Pellaprat was more conventionally French, for he was an ambitious man intent on acquiring as many public offices as he could under the new dispensation. It is a characteristic of our country, people do love to hold public office. In the *Ancien Regime*, the middle classes used to collect them with the passion of an antiquarian putting together a cabinet of curiosities, and there was a period during the revolution when the lower orders thought to make good their arrears in this respect until they realized how dangerous it was. I never understood it myself. Why put yourself in the public eye when most of what matters takes place in private?

"Perhaps we may proceed," said Pellaprat, "now that we all know who we are?"

"I am a young man," I countered. "I only have the haziest notion who I am."

There was a laugh I knew all too well from the back of the church, but the rest of the congregation remained silent except for one or two tuts of disapproval.

"You would do well to curb your facetious manner, Citizen Darbon. We have serious matters to discuss here." The mayor was right. I doubted the gravity of the proceedings, but it wouldn't do Marie-Jeanne any good if I kept making her laugh. Power never likes laughter, small power still less, and the reception accorded my quip suggested I would win no friends among the general population with badinage. "The new representative of the departmental executive directorate is due this morning and we need to be able to provide him with a full report on what is happening in our commune. This meeting has been called to establish exactly what it is you are doing here and ascertain whether it accords with the values of the revolution."

My heart sank a little. Explaining the meridian project had proved complicated in the past and there was little hope I could expect much in the way of Marie-Jeanne's quick wit from my interrogators, let alone the suspicious minds behind me. As if to confirm my misgivings, Citizen Gabadou began fulminating again, grumbling in a way that gave the impression he was trying to eat his own teeth. From what I gathered, he seemed of a mind that I was some sort of spy. I suppose I was in a way. Certainly I was part of a project set upon stealing away the narrow world in which these people had lived until then, reforming them whether they wanted to be reformed or not. I was not unlike Etienne, really. But I'm getting ahead of myself.

When Citizen Gabadou had finished, I began again my by-now well-rehearsed account of the meridian project, taking care to avoid grandiose declarations of rationality, but emphasizing the essential idealism of the plan.

"I appreciate that the techniques we use may seem mysterious to you and what we don't understand can be frightening, a kind of sinister magic. But the magic of this triangulation I have explained is that by making great measurements, we can make small measurements that will benefit everybody, changing human relationships so that men can no longer take advantage of one another. Of course, you will not see the new weights and measures enacted immediately. There is nothing to fear. Everything will be done in due course and with due process. But in time you will see how it liberates you. And you will also see other benefits, for the measurements we make will allow greater precision in mapping, which in turn will mean that we will be able to define the nearby frontiers more precisely, thus making you more secure."

"Ramond will be pleased."

I didn't see who said this, it came from behind my back, but the comment had several members of the audience tittering.

"We don't need measures," said somebody else. "We got our own measures as work for us."

"Don't want maps either. We know where we're going when we go there. Maps only help people who don't know where they're going, strangers. You don't want strangers knowing where they're going. If they know where they're going, they won't hire guides. That's maps for you."

"And the government. They get maps, they know where you are, they know what you got."

"It's not just maps." For a moment I'd forgotten which was Citizen Dalbaret's good eye and wasn't sure which way to look, then I realized he was glowering at the back of the church. "It's drawings too. He was doing her portrait."

"There's nothing wrong in that," said Marie-Jeanne.

"Silence, you," said Citizen Pellaprat. "You forget. Only the heads of households can speak in public meetings."

"So much for the revolution," said Marie-Jeanne. "It's the same rules as before."

"Then perhaps I can speak on my daughter's behalf," said Berenguer. But it was not to be. Something about the idea of her having her portrait done had agitated everybody. As the villagers understood the import of what the factor had seen, everybody began speaking at once.

"Portraits!"

"That child's too free."

"Nobody ever made my picture."

"Knows how to exercise her freedom too."

"It's not her station to be having drawings done of her."

"Not by a tax inspector."

"Getting above herself again."

"No, he's a treasure hunter. We've seen them, walking all over."

"Any daughter of mine."

"He's not from round here."

"Come hunting for witches."

"We know how to make people move on."

"Found one of them all right."

"Give her a good whipping."

"Citizens! Citizens!"

Citizen Pellaprat could citizen all he liked, these particular citizens had found their voice and weren't about to relinquish it so readily. The triumvirate had got to their feet, but nobody was listening to them anymore. How it would all have ended, I do not know, for the meeting was brought to a close by a double intervention. The first did not look good for me. The second saved my skin, though its agent would soon entail my risking that same skin in a more targeted manner.

The church doors crashed open and half a dozen armed men entered. It's remarkable the calming effect a blunderbuss can have on an agitated mob. No shots were fired, but sight of the flared muzzle of the first man's gun was enough to silence the commotion. The intruders had no uniforms, but my heart sank for a second time that day when I saw they were wearing cockades, like the louts I had encountered in Vauriennes.

"We hear you've caught a spy," said blunderbuss. Nobody hesitated. They all turned to me, some helpfully pointing me out in case there was any doubt. "Well done, citizens. No need for any committee work. We'll do the job quick enough. Take him."

Not again! The preceptor at my college had often expressed the opinion that I was born to be hanged, but I hadn't thought his percipience carried so far. First Vauriennes, now Tauzet. Perhaps I ought to stay away from churches. I just had time to see Citizens Gabadou, Dalbaret, and Pellaprat swiftly sitting down behind their table, evidently ready to resign such authority as they had enjoyed until that moment, then I was seized and being bundled toward the church door, the only people making any attempt to interfere being Berenguer and Marie-Jeanne.

The second intervention was less noisy, but the consequences were, if anything, even more spectacular. The way out was barred by a young, well-dressed man with handsome features and startling green eyes. He was wearing a beaver-felt bicorne pinned with a silk tricolor cockade.

"What happens here, citizens?" he asked. "I believe you are expecting me. I come from the executive directorate."

The words were simple enough, but their impact was complex. If the people of Tauzet had been sub-dued before, their silence deepened now, cumbered with shock. Even the Cazalets seemed taken aback. After what I had seen of her, I wouldn't have expected Marie-Jeanne to be taken aback by anything very much.

"Citizen Cazalet," said the young man, smiling at Berenguer before graciously inclining his head toward Marie-Jeanne. "And you, Marie, I trust all is well with you and your goats."

Neither of the Cazalets replied. The directorate's agent turned to the militiamen. They still held me fast but had halted their precipitate rush toward the door.

"He's a spy, citizen," said blunderbuss from behind his lackeys.

"And how do you know this?" The affable smile never faltered, but there was authority in his regard and in his voice.

"He has been seen with strange instruments. He points them at places. Then he writes things down. And he walks all over the hills looking at the land."

"He's no farmer," said one of the men beside me. "You can see that just by looking at him. And he's not from round here."

The young man turned his green eyes on me. They really were most remarkable, flecked with specks of amber near the iris and darkening to a deep-sea green beside the white, but it wasn't the moment to be admiring the color of his eyes.

"I am an assistant surveyor, citizen," I said. "I have been sent ahead, from Paris, to prepare for the arrival of my superiors. It is to do with the new weights and measurements. I am charged with locating stations for measuring the meridian arc. And I have to make a map of this area. The instruments these citizens saw were being used to that purpose."

"Ah, yes," he said. "I have heard of it. A most excellent project."

A most excellent project indeed. I had never been happier to hear such words.

———✦———

"Of course, they're right in a way."

"You think you're too free?"

She pulled a face.

"No, right about mistrusting you. You and this new measure of yours. The measures we have match us. The ones you want match something inside your head."

"And nature."

"A piece of nature that's too big to grasp."

It was the evening after the brouhaha in the church. We were in the Cazalets' cottage, Berenguer, Marie-Jeanne, and myself, sitting at the kitchen table eating a ragout of lard, lentils, and bell beans.

"The old system grew over a long time," said Berenguer. "It means something. It's tied into our lives. It's what generations of people negotiated among themselves."

"And it locks them into themselves," I said. "It's like a language nobody else speaks. They can't make a meaningful trade with other people because nobody measures things the same way."

"But all the ways come from things they understand," said Marie-Jeanne. "Different fields have different yields. It's how long the harvest takes, not how long the field is. Size doesn't reckon the work or the reward. The length of a foot, a stride, a forearm varies. But everyone knows what they mean. Everybody's got an arm and a leg. These are real things. The day's work and what it brings. Things pegged to bits of your body are part of you. You want to take all that away and replace it with a number."

"We don't want to take anything away though. We want to give them liberty."

"It's the 'we' that worries them," said Berenguer. "You heard what Sergi said about maps and the government. They're frightened outsiders are going to take control of things they controlled themselves until now."

A week before, I would have resented their contentions, but given the Cazalets' goodwill, my intellectual insecurity was allayed. The debate was even welcome. It made me decide what I really believed. I was lucky to room with such intelligent, hospitable people. Imagine the conversation had I been lodging with one of the other village notables! Citizen Dalbaret would be spitting in my soup, Citizen Gabadou's expostulations might well have blinded me with spittle, and Citizen Pellaprat would be examining my spit to see if it fit with revolutionary principles.

"But you don't see how important the changes are?" I asked.

"We see it," said Marie-Jeanne. "That's why we're arguing. The way people measure things is a way of thinking, a way of life. You want everybody to think and live the same way."

"But that's what revolutions do," I said, surprising myself, for it was only in articulating the idea that I discovered I had it.

"It wasn't a good idea telling them it was magic," said Berenguer, topping up our beakers with *clairet*. "This triangulation that you do."

"But it is magical."

"Not like they understand magic."

"Then they must be brought to a better understanding. Was that why they were upset about the portrait? Is that some kind of magic too?"

"Of a sort," said Marie-Jeanne. "They're not used to art happening. There's the church. And woodcuts and etchings in the gazettes. But the likeness of real people, people they know. That's from another world. They don't see much difference between the picture and the person. The Virgin they see in the church *is* The Virgin. So it's like you were making more of me."

I could live with that, but I guess it might be scary for people who felt there was already too much Marie-Jeanne for comfort. There were two other matters preying on my mind after the day's events, subjects I hesitated to raise. But the conversation was going so swimmingly.

"And what about Ramond," I said. "What did they mean about him being pleased when I spoke about frontiers?"

The conversation sank.

—◦◦◦—

BERENGUER AND Marie-Jeanne looked at one another. There was a long silence, not a happy one.

"He may as well know," said Berenguer, pushing aside his bowl. "He'll be back soon. Somebody will say something sooner or later." He seemed embarrassed, a forthright man caught dissembling. His daughter nodded and Berenguer turned to me. "My son is not a shepherd."

"That's not a crime," I said, hoping to bring a bit of buoyancy back into the room.

"No, but other things are. Even if people here don't see them like that. It is our custom for the oldest child to inherit everything. To keep the family property together, you understand. Boy or girl, the eldest gets it all. The younger ones have a choice. They can stay in the family home as a dependent. Or they can leave and live without land. Which means poverty, working as a day laborer. Or they can do like Ramond. They make other arrangements."

Silence elbowed its way in again. I spooned up my last bean.

"And the arrangements Ramond has made," I prompted. "They are a problem?"

"Not here, not in the village. But other people might think so. You know, for many years, we had little contact with the people in the plain. We were closer to them across the border. They speak the same language, live the same lives, work the same resources. The frontier's not a natural boundary. It's not even fixed. And it's certainly not impassable. It's often easier to go south than cross into the next valley. We've all got contacts over there, families who have known each other for generations. When governments try to control the price or supply of things, they create a business opportunity. Sugar, tobacco, salt. Sometimes guns, iron, bed linen. Can be anything really. Whatever the market demands. Books are profitable now, books printed here that the Spanish don't want their people to read."

"You're talking contraband? Ramond is a smuggler?"

"The term we prefer is trafficking."

In those days, the Pyrenees were a place apart with a different definition of what was criminal. Smuggling was fine, at a pinch you could get away with killing French officials, but point a theodolite at a mountain and you were in no end of trouble.

"He's not a *miquelet*," said Marie-Jeanne, as if anxious to defend her brother from an unjust accusation. "He doesn't bother travelers or rob anyone. And he works on his own. He's not with one of those big outfits you see with the mules. Just him and his pack. It's mainly books into Spain and *piasters* into France. But a well-regulated border, well, it's not something anyone here would really welcome."

They were surprisingly defensive. I felt that, despite their protestations, they were uneasy about Ramond. Perhaps they simply feared the consequences if he was caught. In any case, I'd already ruined the evening. I might as well satisfy my curiosity on the second point.

"And Citizen Vidal?" I said, naming the young man with green eyes whose timely arrival had saved me from the militia. "He is clearly known here, yet everybody seemed shocked to see him walk in like that."

"You better ask him about that," said Berenguer, picking up his book. Marie-Jeanne started clearing the table. The conversation had drowned. I went out to the barn to consult with Molly.

—⁓—

MARIE-JEANNE WAS distant the next day, but did not object when I suggested a break from mapping. Instead we would check sightlines from stations that might be triangulated against the Pech de Tauzet. It was a wasted day though.

We climbed the *pech* first, leaving the goats brows-ing at its base. Given the great distances involved in triangulating a meridian arc, visibility between sta-tions is paramount. The definitive survey would use parabolic reflectors to identify distant elevations, but for our purposes a white signal cloth would do. We duly installed a tripod of tall poles on the *pech* and tied a sheet of uncut muslin to it to make a beacon that would be visible from all angles.

We had a stiff walk to the first potential station, upward of an hour excluding detours entailed by the goats' incorrigible curiosity, and there was no path to the top, so we had to scramble up through scrub and loose scree. But when we reached the summit, we could see nothing on the *pech*. The weather was calm, there was no wind that might have blown the beacon over, and the air was clear. I could make out a bird of prey circling the peak, but nothing white, not even a flapping cloth. Even through the telescope, I couldn't detect anything.

Somewhat dispirited, we descended the hill and trudged back to the *pech*. The goats didn't mind, but Marie-Jeanne looked downcast. I tried to make light of the abortive expedition, telling her it was the way of these things, that no scientific project could expect to go smoothly all the time. It didn't help though. She was withdrawn, almost sulky, preoccupied with her own concerns.

Once we had climbed the *pech* again, we saw why the signal had been invisible. It had been demolished. The poles were smashed to kindling and the cloth had been meticulously ripped into narrow strips that were scattered about the ground, useless for any-thing but the most rudimentary ligatures. Clearly my speech in the church had not been persuasive. This was deliberate mischief. In the future, I would have to ask Marie-Jeanne to remain on one summit with the reflecting signal while I went to the next to test the sighting.

We were halfway back to the farm when a figure on horseback emerged from behind a copse. Marie-Jeanne was immediately alert, but there was no danger. The rider was Etienne Vidal, the directorate's agent. Marie-Jeanne made a shrill trilling noise with her tongue that brought the goats into line behind her. I was mildly peeved. She might have done this earlier when they were wandering off delaying our progress. Vidal greeted us graciously, but Marie-Jeanne didn't reply. She pursed her lips, whistled once, then hurried off, the goats trotting after her, heads held high with alarm. He watched her go, then dismounted to walk beside me. I apologized for her behavior, saying she was in a strange mood, and explained about our disappointment with the signal.

"A charmingly volatile young lady," he said complacently. "I am sorry to hear about your setback. It is to be expected though. They are a poor sort of people here. They like strangers who pay for a service, then leave. But they don't like outsiders settling and they don't like the idea of change, no matter how miserable their lot."

"So I was given to understand. I have not had occasion to thank you for yesterday."

He waved my thanks aside.

"The least I could do for a fellow man of science. I fear your task here will not be easy. But at least you do not suffer the usual boredom a surveyor experiences, confined to a mountaintop with no one to converse with. You have an engaging companion."

He was still gazing after the departing figure of Marie-Jeanne, though I didn't pay much heed to this at the time. I was too pleased to be acknowledged as a brother in science. He really was a charming man and he clearly had a good brain.

"You are also a geographical engineer?" I asked.

That would explain his familiarity with the meridian project.

"An engineer, yes, but of a different sort. I am the local *Inspecteur des Eaux et Forêts*. I'm on a tour to supervise the wardens. And to assess the damage done by that creature there."

He nodded toward the village. For a moment I thought he meant Marie-Jeanne, but then I saw that one of the goats had plucked up courage to linger and strip some bark from a May tree.

"And the directorate?"

"What? Oh, that, too. These are exciting times for young men like us. It wouldn't do to let the opportunities pass us by." We were silent a moment, Etienne gazing at the goat, then he added: "I think I shall stay here awhile."

"You have found a welcome then?"

"I have found accommodation. I wouldn't go so far as to say I am welcome." He said this equably, as if it was all one with him. "I am lodging with Citizen Gabadou."

I couldn't quite suppress an involuntary gasp. It was hard to picture this beguiling young man with his beautiful green eyes hobnobbing with the priest.

"You are surprised?" he asked, turning aside from his inspection of the goat.

"Citizen Gabadou seems a somewhat splenetic individual."

Etienne smiled.

"He is, but he has the largest house in the village and keeps the best table. One must make oneself as comfortable as one can." He glanced at the goat again. This time she got the message and scampered off to join Marie-Jeanne. "Welcome or not," he added.

No matter how intelligent the Cazalets were, it was agreeable to converse with an educated man again. I did not, therefore, want to alienate Etienne, but I was still curious about his reception the previous day, so I took the risk and asked him about it.

"Yes," he said, untroubled by my prying. "Yes, they know me. I was here before. That's why I know how they feel toward outsiders. Only then I was neither an inspector, nor a representative of the authorities. That would explain their surprise. They must be a little uneasy."

He seemed quite satisfied by the situation. When he explained, I could understand both their surprise and, perhaps, his satisfaction. Etienne's father was a wealthy merchant in the nearby city of Limoux, a draper and vintner with extensive properties throughout the region. Prior to his studies, Etienne had been sent to Tauzet to manage his father's holdings in the vicinity and familiarize himself with the practice of business. During this time he had conceived an affection for Marie-Jeanne. He was quite open about this, as if it was a commonplace admission. The liaison had been ill-viewed, both by his father and the villagers. But the young couple had persisted in their romance and even planned to live together for a probationary year, as was the custom in these parts. It was only when Etienne had been informed that, if he proceeded, his father would disinherit him and the villagers would subject the wedding to a *charivari,* that he had desisted and broken off the engagement.

"A *charivari*?" I said. "That's like a carnival?"

"As noisy," he said, smiling at my naivete. "But less benign. Its purpose is to express disapproval of a misalliance. And marriage to an outsider counts as that. Pots, pans, a travesty of an orchestra, the ritual humiliation of the victims. It can come to violence, too, if you don't pay them off."

"And you gave way to the threat?"

The smile faltered, but only briefly.

"Let us say I concluded that a woman from the city, one who met with my father's approval, would be a more appropriate spouse for a man like me."

"And you do not regret your decision?" I was more shocked than I allowed.

"Oh, there are always regrets," he said. "I'm not proud of what I did. Leaving her like that. I have my regrets. But like all things in life, it's a question of how you handle them. Now, to this project in which you are engaged, my friend." He took me by the elbow as if we were old familiars. I was flattered, both by the implicit amity and his interest in my work. "Your endeavors might meet less resistance if you could bring the villagers to a better understanding of what you are doing." We really were of like minds in many ways. I had used almost exactly the same words the evening before. "What I would suggest is a demonstration of triangulation. I have the authority to assemble the village. If you were to show them how you go about making a measurement using this technique . . ."

"A better understanding?"

"Yes, a better understanding."

—⁓—

ONE THING was better understood, at least, the other "accident" of history Marie-Jeanne had mentioned. She had set herself against village opinion and then been spurned. I was naive, but not that naive. I knew people were capable of hating an alliance, then becoming resentful if one of theirs was deemed unfit for the match, even if they had been instrumental in ending the affair. Now she had made matters worse by taking up with another unwelcome outsider.

Two days later, standing in the middle of a field on the fringes of Tauzet, the outsider was all too well aware of his status as an interloper. Etienne had been true to his word in this, at least. Everyone in the village was present, as well as many who had been elsewhere, working in the woods, mines, and rural manufactories. They had gathered on the edge of the field and they didn't look happy about it. The only friendly faces were those belonging to Etienne, Berenguer, and Marie-Jeanne. I had not spoken with the Cazalets about Etienne's revelations, but they were not given to harboring grudges, and if the damage done by my inquiries was not quite undone, I sensed the indiscretion had been forgiven.

Etienne was walking up and down in front of the crowd, his hands clasped together, like a child excited by an outing. He kept flashing bright smiles at the people he passed, not in the least put out by the sullen response. I envied him his capacity for ignoring hostility. At length, he concluded the assembly was sufficient for the demonstration to proceed and he announced, in a clear, steady voice, the purpose of the gathering. He then turned to me and waved me forward. I felt like a trained bear invited to dance and about as willing.

"We are here today," I said, trying to sound as relaxed as Etienne, "so that I can reassure you about the work I am doing. The equipment you have seen me using has excited some suspicion. But you should not be frightened by it. These are simply tools for measuring things. This one is called a theodolite. It's an instrument for measuring the angles of intersecting lines. When we know how sharp an angle is, we can calculate certain distances without having to measure them all on foot. What I propose is that you should select three visible points that form a triangle. We shall measure the angles at two of the points and the distance between them, then I can calculate the distance of the third point. Who would care to choose the points?"

Nobody. The villagers shifted uneasily, carefully avoiding meeting my gaze. I had warned the Cazalets against participating and Etienne knew better than to propose his services. For a moment, it seemed the experiment would progress no further. Then a man stepped forward.

"Citizen Dalbaret?" I could have done without that, but it was better than nobody. "Would you care to designate the three points?"

"It can be anything?" the factor asked.

"Anything we can all see, yes."

Smirking at me, a malicious gleam in his eyes, he turned to the crowd.

"I designate . . . Ferran, Theo, and Mateu."

I didn't need to ask who they were. Ferran, Theo, and Mateu were protesting vigorously. From their clothing, they appeared to be foresters, charcoal-burners most like, for their forearms and necks were laced with seams of ingrained grime, and their shoulders and trouser legs were blackened with soot.

"I had intended some fixture," I said. "Something immovable, like trees and rocks."

"They're all fixtures," said the factor, enjoying his little moment of revenge.

"Yes, but . . ."

"No buts. You said anything."

"Come on, you three," said Etienne, briskly ushering the unwilling stations of my triangle forward. Ordering them about like that did not seem wise. These were the very people most likely to resent his role as inspector of forests, the outsider enforcing rules governing their activities. He shouldn't treat them so high-handedly, especially since they were far from being ideal triangulation points. There was no avoiding it though. I had said "anything" and if I was to win the confidence of the villagers, I could not balk at their first proposition.

The three men shuffled forward. I explained that they should stand apart at a good distance from one another so that they formed a triangle. When they had taken up their respective positions, I called for another volunteer. Again the ground became an engrossing object of contemplation, then a voice from the back of the crowd shouted: "Citizen Dalbaret!"

There was laughter from all save the factor, who looked like his head might be about to burst, which wouldn't do my reputation any good at all. Having volunteered the others though, he could not very well refuse. I explained the functioning of the perambulator and had him measure in *toises* the baseline between Theo and Mateu. Ferran flinched when I aimed the theodolite at him from Mateu's corner, and Theo didn't like it any better. Mateu looked quite chipper until he realized he was the first target from Theo's corner. But all three survived the experience. Telling them to remain in place, I rapidly made my calculations and informed the crowd how far Ferran was from each of the others. The factor walked the lines and grudgingly confirmed my calculation. The people were watching closely now, listening carefully, but they still looked doubtful.

"I shall now calculate how far that tree is," I announced. I measured the angles from Ferran and Mateu, and again calculated the distance correctly. "So you see," I said. "This tool is nothing sinister. I have had these men in my sights twice and they have come to no harm. It is simply a way of establishing distances without having to pace them out or measure them with rods or chains. You really have nothing to fear."

All eyes were on me. They were impressed by my feat. I was momentarily distracted though. Marie-Jeanne was conversing with a young man I hadn't seen before, a strongly built fellow with a pistol in his waistband, and a large, empty pack on his shoulders. He was a gloomy-looking individual, but if you ignored the frowning, which had permanently creased his forehead, the resemblance to Berenguer was obvious. Ramond had returned.

"You are clever, Citizen Darbon." It was the priest speaking, the first time I had seen him give utterance without spluttering, but his coolness was no less vituperative. "Perhaps a little too clever. We are a simple people here. We do not take to cleverness. It smacks of a kind of magic."

That word again! It was too late though. It was out and the people were looking at each other, nodding and muttering, agreeing that there was something menacing about a man who could determine distances he hadn't walked. This was a kind of occult learning. As the crowd broke up, Etienne approached, a twist of sympathy touching his habitual smile.

"Not quite as I had hoped," he said. "They really are incorrigible. But we shall correct them. Even if it kills some of them in the process. When great changes are afoot, you can't let the riffraff get in the way. But you look like you need a drink, my friend. Come."

—◦◦◦—

I NEVER did dine with the priest. No matter how flexible his beliefs, his distaste for me was indomitable, but judging by his cellar, Citizen Gabadou treated his tummy very well indeed. The frustration of the morning had already been blotted out and Etienne was opening a second bottle from the priest's stock when I expressed some mild reservations about his referring to the local people as riffraff. It intimated a sentiment that hardly seemed to fit with revolutionary ideals.

"Ideals are in the nature of objectives," said Etienne, pouring generous measures of wine. "The revolution acts in the name of the people. For now, that is enough. Indeed, it is all that is possible. You saw what they're like. An uneducated rabble wedded to superstition. They have been isolated far too long. They're centuries behind educated men like you and me. We are the men of the future. And we must put our learning at the service of the people. No question of that. But we mustn't let the people inhibit our learning. In due course, we can improve them. As a man of science, you should recall that matter is neither created nor destroyed, only transformed. The transformation will come. But for the present, the illusion of liberty is all they can know."

"You think they will be content with that?" I asked, drinking deeply. It really was very good wine. Even at my employer's table in Paris, I had rarely tasted anything of comparable quality.

"The French are a submissive people," said Etienne, matching me, swig for swig. "But they don't like to be told so. As long as they believe they are free agents, they will do what is required of them. We must guide them though. Now, yourself, have you acquired any preferment yet?"

"You mean related to the new disposition? No, I am a man of science, not politics."

"You understand that nobody loves a neutral," he said, looking at me closely. "You will have to declare yourself one way or another."

"We are not at war," I said.

"Not yet," he said. "But that will come. In another sense, though, we are at war even now. A war against ignorance and injustice. Indeed, in your present role, you are already engaged in that war, fighting superstition and intolerance. And you had better get used to the idea. A surveyor standing on top of a mountain may think he is above the fray, but he is also a perfect target."

"I confess, I have had some doubts about that."

"Being a target?" Our glasses were empty again, but only briefly.

"No, the science." I had not forgotten what the Cazalets had said. "Or its objectives, at least. It's not just the surveyor they're sniping at. It's the things we seek to produce too. People don't like the idea of this new measure. By excluding everything that is qualitative and establishing a purely numerical relation between things, we are creating a system adapted to savants, not peasants. The savants expect people to become more like themselves. But is it not a mistake to believe everyone wants to live in a savants' utopia? People are not uniform."

"Nonsense," he said, slopping wine on the table. Our gestures were already considerably more expansive than is customary, even in the south. "Universality is vital to the revolution. This nation is in the vanguard of history. But to be a nation, it requires uniformity. Not just politically, but in its customs too. Until now, daily life has defined measurement, which is why it's chaotic. When the world is chaotic someone has to construct a new order so people know where they are. That's your job, mine, the work of every right-minded, educated man. We must redefine everything, time, distance, weight, volume, just as we define what people believe. That is history's gift to our generation and it will be our gift to posterity."

It was young man's talk, grand ideas buoyed up by hot air and a lot of wine, and I was loving it. I hadn't realized how much I had missed the free play of pure thought and liked Etienne all the more for bringing me back to the game of ideas. And the liking prompted me to warn him.

"You know, I am not the only vulnerable target," I said, leaning toward him, a conspiratorial elder dispensing wise advice. "You should be prudent in your dealings with the people. Those foresters you forced to participate this morning. You must know that they see you as a threat, the agent of an alien administration. Like the magistrates and tax collectors. It would be as well not to aggravate matters by inspiring more animosity."

Etienne made a dismissive sound.

"I'm not frightened of them," he said. "You know, there are twelve sheep here for every man, woman, and child. Imagine! Through proximity alone, these people are almost sheep themselves."

"Yet you were worried enough to move on before."

The thought pained me, for his craven mistreatment of Marie-Jeanne hurt my desire to like the man. Etienne seemed to sense as much and sought to mollify me. He refilled my glass.

"But then I did not enjoy the positions I hold now. Now I can do what I want, say what I want, take what I want. They don't dare touch me. And if they try, I always have this."

Lifting the side vent of his waistcoat, he revealed the stock of a small pistol tucked into his belt, the second such gun I had seen since breakfast. It seemed a lot for one day.

"You would use that thing?"

"I know how," he said.

"That's not what I asked," I said.

"Then, yes, if necessary, I would use it. You can't be too squeamish in times of turmoil. And you, would you not use a gun when it was necessary?"

"I don't know how," I said.

"That's not what I asked," he said.

"Well, maybe. If pushed."

"We'll drink to that then," said Etienne. "If pushed, Citizen Darbon is willing!"

It seemed a reasonable toast, though by that stage of the proceedings I suspect we would have been ready to celebrate the beauty of our pretty pink toes if somebody had proposed as much.

"You mustn't be too soft, you know," he said, emptying the bottle. "You've got to run with the world or it will leave you behind. The direction we're running now is toward violence. The symptoms are everywhere, all around us, in the heart of every man you meet. But on the other side of violence lies the new world where the state will shape the minds of men. It's no longer enough for men to act as the state demands. They must think as the state demands too. They must become what the state demands. In such circumstances, it is preferable to be among those doing the shaping than among those being shaped. And for that, we must survive the period of violence."

"You are a long way from the centers of power here," I said, adding to the puddle of wine on the table as I endeavored to indicate the great distance I had in mind, though by then I doubt I had very much in mind at all. "Shaping sheep and goats won't win you much eminence."

"You may be wrong there, my friend. Every detail counts. The depredations of the goats on the forests are considerable. You saw that creature stripping bark the other day. That was just one goat, one bush. But there are thousands of goats and we have noble woods here too. When war comes, the shipyards at Toulon will need timber. The man who can guarantee a supply will be in a position of power."

"The people are fond of their goats," I said, though in truth, I was thinking as much of myself as the people, for I had learned to like Marie-Jeanne's charges, despite their willful nature. Or maybe it was because of it. I secretly admired their capricious independence and inebriation made my admiration fonder. "And they need them during the summer. They'll fight to keep them."

"You are a sentimentalist. Nothing is sacred. Utility is the only value. The pursuit of perfection justifies everything."

"Does perfection exist?" I asked. "We're trying to weigh the world, yet it won't hold still. Worse, the closer we look the less perfect it seems. All bumps and boils and fissures and scars. Curves that don't accord with classical perfection. Mountains that skew our instruments. And men are much the same, are they not, full of faults and unpredictable defects? Perfecting them is going to be the devil's own job."

"That's what I have been telling you. There's work to be done here. It's a colossal task. Best do the work than be worked. Come on, drink. People like us, we can have everything in the new order. We should not shy from taking what we want. But you've got to want it. It's no good ending up with regrets it's too late to remedy. And when you can remedy your regrets, you should do so."

The third bottle was opened and our scholarly discourse deteriorated considerably.

I STAGGERED across the threshold and embraced Berenguer.

"I love you," I declared.

Berenguer turned aside, probably to avoid becoming intoxicated by the fumes I was giving off, but I seem to recall a small smile passing across his lips.

Marie-Jeanne appeared beside her father, looking diaphanous, in large measure because I couldn't see her very clearly.

"I love you too," I cried.

Unhooking myself from her father's neck, I careened off into the kitchen, where I was deftly caught by the table. I was full of admiration for its agility. I had thought it inanimate, but it had done a complicated dance across the kitchen floor in order to catch me.

Another shadow passed across my line of view.

"And you," I said. "I love you too. Who are you?"

"Your taste in men has not improved, sister."

"I'm not your sister," I said. "Am I?" I was none too sure by this stage.

The last thing I remember was being put to bed by Marie-Jeanne.

"Bad man," I said. "Glad you didn't marry him."

Even at the time, despite the parlous state of my mental faculties, I was puzzled by this statement. But as they say, *in vino veritas*, and something in my befuddled mind had discerned an aspect of Etienne my conscious self was earnestly trying to suppress. Then I passed out.

"Forget it. It was nothing. You were . . . very amusing. And very friendly. Very, very friendly. Most men become less likable with drink."

I didn't ask for details. The idea that I was likable in any condition was enough to silence me, all except my head, which was pounding in a manner I imagined might be audible outside as well as in. Despite Marie-Jeanne's acceptance of my apology, I still had a strong urge to hide my face in my hands and start howling. What had I been thinking? Was I capable of thought? You see what I mean about imbecility. Getting stewed, then reeling out of the night proclaiming your tender feelings for anyone who happens to cross your path is not indicative of a fully functioning intellect. A man of science? A savant? I was about as sapient as the plate of porridge waiting for me on the kitchen table.

When Berenguer and Ramond returned from their chores, I repeated my apologies. Berenguer smiled his wise, forgiving smile, and said everybody was young once. His youth notwithstanding, Ramond looked less convinced. I held out my hand, introducing myself as somebody other than his sister. It was a moment before he accepted the handshake and only then at the prompting of his father. After that, he ate his porridge quickly, ignoring my attempts to draw him into conversation, though that might have been for reasons other than boorishness, since I was still in an advanced state of decay, and my remarks were about as stimulating as a compost heap.

"You must excuse him," said Berenguer after Ramond had left to go about his business. "My son has never been very open." He lifted the lid of the settle beside the table and brought out a bottle. "I wasn't mother enough for him. Even Marie-Jeanne, and he adores her, could not make up the want inside him."

"I tried," she said. "But I was a child too. You can't be a mother and a child. And I was perhaps too free, too full of myself."

"Never that," said Berenguer. "You mustn't say such things. Leave it to the gossips. No, I'm not sure anybody could help. I think he blames himself. His mother's death, I mean. It eats at him. You remember how upset he was when that ewe died giving birth? And since he took up this new trade, it has been worse. The last few years. He's angry all the time. Here, drink this. It will help."

He had poured a dash of clear liquid into a small cup.

"Help with Ramond?"

"No, with your head. Drink it in one and don't breathe."

My head needed all the help it could get. I downed the contents of the cup. The advice about breathing was superfluous. I couldn't. Indeed for a moment I feared the draft was designed to help my head by blowing a hole in the back of it to relieve the pressure. But when the spirit bludgeoned its way into my internal organs it did make a difference. I doubted it would do much for the head, that was beyond redress, but the rest of me felt vaguely integrated.

Nothing more was said about Ramond, nor was the subject of Etienne broached. My declaration when Marie-Jeanne was putting me to bed was not alluded to and, out of respect for the Cazalets' discretion, I decided not to mention the broken engagement again. I still wondered at myself though. The addled announcement that my new friend was a bad man must have come from somewhere, but apart from the fact that he had been less than gentlemanly in his conduct toward Marie-Jeanne, I could see no reason to condemn him. Yet there was something there, something that did not quite cohere.

In the following days, when we were out mapping and scouting triangulation stations, we happened to encounter Etienne quite frequently. He kept popping up in the most unexpected places. Whenever he was there, Marie-Jeanne wouldn't say a word. I could understand it, but to maintain a semblance of civility I would chat to Etienne, as if her frosty silence wasn't crackling in the air like cold lightning. There was something wrong though. I had the feeling he was only half listening to me and I didn't like the way he looked at Marie-Jeanne. He had admitted he had regrets. But he wasn't going to make amends by watching her. Certainly not like that. He had to act, do something to redeem himself. And it was this thought that bothered me most. Only later did I realize I was jealous, not of anything concrete that existed between them, but because he had known her before I did.

For somebody who had claimed he would be a connoisseur of human absurdity this was an emotion of impeccable stupidity.

When left to our own devices, Marie-Jeanne and I were easy together. The talk was never personal, seldom serious, but as we made our way between stations, or sketched a tranche of land, or waited while the goats took their own measure of the terrain, we told tales to pass the time, tales that I now see fostered that appreciation of absurdity we had resolved to cultivate. I told her about the famous astronomer, Jérôme Lalande, and his eccentric appetites, how he would eat bugs and insects, reporting that caterpillars tasted like peaches, while spiders resembled hazelnuts. I felt a little guilty mocking the great man but consoled myself with the thought that the foibles of the famous bring them closer to us, so that even the most august personages and abstruse ideas are approachable. Marie-Jeanne told me about the "frictioners" in the spa towns of the Pyrenees, where women who had difficulty conceiving would have their bellies rubbed by professional scrubbers to encourage fecundity in the womb. We did not delve into the ribald connotations. We did not need to. The idea of kneading fertility into a tummy was delectable enough in a world where every bull, buck, and ram could do the job without manual assistance. Yet the nonsense we told each other was not without meaning. With our silly talk, we were unwittingly making a mental map of the human heart. Triangulating tales of the absurd, we were identifying what was not absurd, defining what we valued without speaking it aloud.

I also tried teasing her with some of Alcuin's classic conundrums from the *Propositiones ad Acuendos Juvenes*, like the famous problem of getting a wolf, a goat, and a cabbage across a river without the wolf eating the goat or the goat eating the cabbage. Needless to say, she got them all. It was a bit irritating actually. She might have made shift to at least pretend she wasn't very quick on the uptake. Mild vexation notwithstanding, I was vaguely aware that these were special days and that, in the course of their procession, something inside me was being processed too.

Walking with Marie-Jeanne, enchanted by her irreverence and perspicacity, I was beguiled into a relationship with the land, not the land of the intellect in which I had reveled during my journey south, that square cut earth diced by straight lines of latitude and longitude, but a more ancient world of winding ways and warped contours, a place of nooks and crannies, impertinent promontories and clandestine dells, the world that resists the attempts of men of science to define it. Quite why or how this happened, I still do not know. All I can say is that affection, for both people and places, is at once inevitable and unaccountable. There is nothing anyone can do about this. Affinity works on us and we must accept it wherever it manifests itself.

It all coalesced one afternoon when Marie-Jeanne showed me her secret place. That sounds like a smutty euphemism. It is in a way, though the hidden parts of her body were to remain unknown, to me at least, for some time to come. It was an exceptionally hot day and we were walking back from a distant hill. The trail was so dry and dusty that even the goats seemed dispirited. But they perked up when Marie-Jeanne made that distinctive whistle she used for calling them to follow and they saw her turn off onto a virtually imperceptible path climbing a narrow valley.

I was too hot and bothered to question where we were going, so simply trailed after the goats, supposing it was a shortcut. But once inside the valley, it became clear that there was no way out the other end, which was sealed by sheer rock. As we approached the foot of the cliff, the goats quickened their pace. Then I heard water. There was no stream, no trace of the meanders that must have carved out the declivity, but the higher we went the louder the sound became. As we neared the top, the valley dipped down, revealing a sheet of rock shining with water and ribboned with dangling fingers of verdant ferns. Lower down the rock face, the water became more copious, widening and deepening to form a heavy silver curtain dropping directly into a broad, teal-blue pool. The goats rushed to the pool's edge to drink.

"But where does it come from?" I asked. "Where does it go?"

"The water? From nowhere to nowhere. It comes out of the rock up there and disappears somewhere down there. It never dries though. Even in the hottest summers. Here, take off anything you don't want to get wet."

She kicked off her clogs and pulled her tunic overhead. Wearing nothing but a flimsy chemise, she started climbing a narrow way to the right of the falls. I only hesitated a moment. Tugging off my boots, I untied my breeches, shed waistcoat and shirt, and followed her. Being abroad in short linen drawers took me back to my days at the orphanage when we were marched to church and would slip away from our supervisors to swim in the bay. It is in moments of escape that we find ourselves, and the language of flight and freedom remains much the same, from our youngest days to our oldest years. Sadly, we tend to

forget this, muzzling ourselves with masks of respect-
ability and vapid precepts about the way things are.

Behind the waterfall there was a shallow cave
sealed by the jalousie of water. It was damp and deliciously fresh on the ledge at the lip of the cave, where
we were filmed with a fine spray that clung to the
skin, drawing together in diamond-like droplets. The
light was preternatural, mantling us in an amphibian
unreality, creatures on the brink, suspended between
elements. Marie-Jeanne held her face up to catch the
moisture between her lips and spread her arms wide,
the dark veins in her biceps glistening like threads of
birch tar. Then she stepped forward and dived through
the waterfall. Again, I only hesitated briefly.

If the cave had been cool and otherworldly, the leap
was of a different order altogether. That spot would
become one of my favorite places, but despite repeated
visits, I shall never forget the sensation of that first
jump, slipping through the shimmering screen into a
flash of bright light and a splash of cold water as I
plunged into the pool below.

Marie-Jeanne had already clambered out on the far
side, her shift plastered tightly to her body, the dark
lozenge between her legs and the cocked eyes of her
startled nipples clearly visible through the thin material. What she saw of me I did not know, nor much
care, for I was too taken up triangulating the raw sen-
suality of her. Then she was off again, tripping up the
path to the parapet and flinging herself through the
water. The goats were used to such hijinks for they
did not flinch when we plashed into the depths of the
pool but continued drinking at its edge and browsing
on the surrounding foliage.

The fourth or fifth time we were racing up to the
cave, I caught Marie-Jeanne by the wrist. It was not

premeditated, just an impulsive act of intimacy, all part of the impish sport. She turned, looked up at me. I leaned forward, kissed her quickly on the lips, then released her, and hurried up to jump. That was all, but I often look back on that day as the moment something was sealed, some promise made, despite everything that was to come between us in the coming months.

That night, the plain table was wrecked. The following night, everything else fell apart.

EARLY NEXT morning I was talking with Berenguer. The money I had brought from Paris was nearly finished. I still had letters of credit, but given my employers' lack of communication, I had begun to doubt the documents' validity. Indeed, had it not been for Etienne's confirmation, I might have concluded the meridian project no longer existed at all, that I had been set adrift, stranded in other men's aborted dreams. Even if that wasn't the case, the administrative chaos entailed by the revolution meant there was no guarantee any additional debt I engaged would be repaid by the government. Not wanting to abuse Berenguer's hospitality, I asked him if he knew anyone who would be interested in buying a mule. He laughed at the idea, said he wouldn't dream of separating me from Molly, and did not doubt any liabilities I contracted would be made good. Then Ramond returned from watering the livestock.

"Your machine," he said, "the table thing. It's broke. And the mule has gone."

He did not sound unduly troubled by the discovery, nor very surprised. His humor had not improved in the preceding days, and he remained gruff and uncommunicative with me, no matter what overtures of friendship I made.

Out in the barn, where the plain table had been stored, we found its remains. The top was intact, but the legs had been hacked off, the spirit level smashed, and the alidade was bent out of shape, well beyond repair for a precision instrument. On the instant though, I was more disturbed by the disappearance of Molly. She had been saved from the knackers, saved from being sold into an uncertain future, and now she had vanished. Not by chance either. Whoever broke the table had opened her stall and, in view of her temperament, taken some pains to shoo her into the night. I was upset, too upset to think clearly, because I interpreted the fact that the gate to the goat pen remained closed in a wholly negative manner.

"Where were you last night?" I said.

Ramond's saturnine features darkened further.

"Here, as you well know."

"You wouldn't suggest Ramond did this," said Berenguer.

I hated to upset the old man, but I really was thrown off-kilter by Molly's disappearance.

"I suggest it would have been easier for someone inside the house to slip out in the night than for someone from outside to risk discovery. I don't have any doubts about you and Marie-Jeanne. But your son has shown every sign of displeasure at my company since he returned."

"Ramond wouldn't do such a thing," said Berenguer. "You didn't, did you?"

He sounded a little desperate. Marie-Jeanne had yet to say a word in her brother's defense, as if she wasn't sure of his innocence either. Ramond didn't reply, just continued to glare at me. Finally, Berenguer spoke again, constrained to fill the awkward silence.

"Ramond is your friend in this," he said. "His employment involves special skills. Like knowing who has passed where and when. He's one of the best trackers in the village. He'll find your mule for you, won't you, Ramond?"

Ramond did not reply, but after a pause that was lengthening into the painful, he nodded his head. It was only later that I realized my conjecture had been unjust. A more positive reading of the evidence would have concluded that the culprit had not disturbed the goats because my presence had not yet put the Cazalets wholly beyond the pale. I was the stranger, the intruder who had to be unsettled and discouraged.

Berenguer had business in the village and Marie-Jeanne had to tend the goats, so Ramond and I were left to ourselves. For obvious reasons, the atmosphere as we set off was not cordial, and we did not speak for some while. Ramond had his eyes trained on the ground, picking out Molly's prints, pausing from time to time when they were crossed by those of other animals.

Despite my suspicions, it was interesting to watch the way he read the ground. We had this in common at least. The origin of the word "survey" means to look down at, notice, guard, watch; it is the act of viewing in detail. With my survey, I was trying to assimilate a landscape, imagining a bird's-eye view of what was below. There was arrogance in this, putting oneself above the world, but it could also be seen as a recognition of nature's vast complexity and the elevation we must attain to comprehend it. Yet what Ramond saw on the ground was indiscernible from the heights to which I aspired. It implied a different type of attentiveness, in which the closer you look, the more you see, revealing vital details that are invisible from above. It was a method that might seduce me into something like religious belief. Pious people often praise their maker rather than celebrating what he made. But if God is anywhere, he is in creation. Paying close attention to the material world, we are also exploring the spiritual.

These may seem strange thoughts to entertain in the circumstances, but I believe my anxiety about Molly was such that I needed to distract myself with abstract speculation. There were bears and wolves in the high country. I hated to think of her being torn apart. More than that though, these meditations were symptomatic of my growing enchantment with landscape and the uneasy feeling that a sense of place is finally more important than factual analysis. The way Ramond followed the tracks on the ground suggested a different engagement with the world. My faith in scientific methods was all bent out of shape, like the alidade in the barn.

After a while we crossed a freshly plowed field where several members of a family were preparing the ground for winter crops, two young women scratching at the furrows with short hoes, a couple of children clearing stones, and an old man with a maimed hand spreading manure. They'd not seen Molly, but Ramond picked up her traces again on the far side of the field.

"He's a grand man, that one," said Ramond as we proceeded. They were the first words he had addressed to me without prompting.

"He certainly seemed venerable," I said, carefully.

"You saw his hand, the missing fingers?"

"An accident in a sawmill?"

"No accident," he said. "He cut them off himself. To avoid conscription into the militia."

He went back to his tracking, but the message was clear. People here would rather cripple themselves than cooperate with the outside world, and I was of that world.

On rising ground, we entered a maze of box, oak, and limestone in which I soon became disoriented. Not knowing where I was made me nervous. If Ramond meant to do away with an unwelcome interloper, there could be no better place for it. He might not even need to do the job himself. If I lost him, I doubted I would find my way out alone. The trees were twisted by wind and twined about large blocks of eroded rock cloaked in a dense blanket of moss. There was no path, only a skein of conflicting ways, crisscrossing one another, weaving back and forth, like a ball of snarled yarn. The light itself seemed tormented by the elements, falling between the trees in tangled knots that flouted the laws of optics. It was as if landscape reflected affiliation, the luminous wonderland of Marie-Jeanne's waterfall contrasted with the dark labyrinth that belonged to her moody brother. But for all my febrile fears and fancies, there was joy there too. In a bright glade at the heart of the maze, we found Molly peacefully cropping purple clover.

I don't think she'd been hugged much in her life and she shied away when I threw my arms about her neck, but she did not seem displeased to see me. When I turned back, half expecting Ramond would have disappeared, I found him watching us, his habitual sardonic expression tempered by a kinder amusement. I apologized for my unjust accusations. He shrugged his shoulders, made a huffing noise, as if to indicate that my qualms were of no interest to him, then turned on his heel. He did not run though. Instead he waited for me at crucial intersections while I coaxed Molly out of the maze. When we emerged, I discovered that his surly attitude toward me was as nothing to the waves of hostility at his disposition.

Etienne was sitting on his horse at the edge of the wood. He really did get everywhere that man. Rather than his smart bicorne, he was wearing a broad brimmed straw hat of the sort more often worn by peasants working in the fields or by genteel women protecting fashionably pale complexions. But the incongruity did not trouble him and he doffed his hat in a most elegant manner. For all my ambiguous feelings toward him, I couldn't quell a twinge of envy. Both the headgear and the gesture were things I would never be able to carry off with such aplomb.

There was no ambiguity about Ramond's reaction. If Marie-Jeanne's reception of Etienne was frosty, the cold fury emanating from Ramond ought to have been enough to knock him off his horse. Even from behind it was palpable. I don't know how Etienne kept his seat, still less how he held his charming smile and steadied the gaze of those lovely green eyes, fixed as they were on a face that was full of hate. It was too much for Ramond. He whirled around and stalked off, leaving the two of us, men of science and outsiders, alone.

"Why do I get the idea that the Cazalets don't care for me," said Etienne, as he turned his horse to inspect Ramond's retreating back. I could not help but contrast our two mounts, his sleek expensive bloodstock and my blowzy old crossbreed.

"You treated her badly," I said.

Molly nudged my elbow with her muzzle. I petted her face, amused at my sentimental folly. I would never exchange her for another animal, no matter what the lineage.

"Maybe I did," he said, turning back to smile at me. "I told you, I am not proud of what I did. I have my regrets."

"You also said that when you can remedy your regrets you should do so."

"I did, indeed. And what would you suggest, my friend?"

"You should speak to her," I said. "You won't make good the wrong you did otherwise."

He eyed me a moment. Those eyes! I am sorry to go on about this, but I only ever saw one other pair of eyes like that. They have become a kind of talisman in my life.

"I will do that," he said, taking up his reins. "Maybe she'll take me to your bathing hole!"

I was speechless with shock, but he just laughed and rode away, as if the suggestion that he had been spying on us was merely a young man's jape, the common currency of friendship. There is nothing so absurd as a jealous lover and it makes matters no easier when the other party is the one with green eyes. I only wish I had better understood the nature of his regrets.

―――

I HAVE tried to keep this chronicle light. Life is heavy enough without memorialists burdening the world with their bad experiences. Indeed I think it should be the task of every maker of things to bring a little lightness into life, even when describing the darkest and weightiest matters. We all know the world can be dark and heavy. We don't need other people making a spectacle of how sensitive they are because they feel it all more acutely than we do. And a light touch helps keep things at one remove, preventing them from over-whelming us. But in some situations, even a connois-seur of human absurdity cannot distance the pain.

The facts.

It was Marie-Jeanne's custom to check on the goats last thing at night. She had been gone some while. Her father and brother were already in bed. I was about to go to bed myself, but having recovered Molly so recently, I decided to follow Marie-Jeanne's example and ensure all was well with my charge. I was approaching the barn when I heard some perplexing sounds, a muffled grunting and scuffling that did not resemble the noises made by the goats. It was dark inside the barn, but when my eyes grew accustomed to the lack of light, I picked out two figures pressed against the stack of hay. Or rather one figure.

Etienne's breeches were wadded at the tops of his riding boots. The pleats of his shirt gussets flapped about his bare buttocks. One hand circled Marie-Jeanne's wrists, pinning them above her head, the other was placed under her chin forcing her head back. Her tunic and chemise were bunched above her waist. Marie-Jeanne bucked and writhed, but Etienne held her firm, pressing himself between her legs, his hips pumping.

Enough said. There are times when facts speak louder than feelings.

FOR ONE insane moment, I almost wished they were making love, that this was a voluntary act on her part. Despite my earlier doubts, despite the shock of the

revelation he had made that afternoon, I did not want
to believe that Etienne was sexually violating Marie-
Jeanne. I did not want him violating her in any way.
I would have welcomed jealousy if it let me believe
their copulation involved no coercion. But the hand at
her throat, the pinioned wrists told a different story.
And Marie-Jeanne's writhing was too convulsive and
contradictory. She wasn't opening up to him. She was
trying to close down. She wasn't taking pleasure. He
was. And the taking was all.

The fight that ensued was a foolish affair, a ruffling
of feathers rather than a real affray. On stage and on
the page these things unfold in a different manner, but
experience suggests most fighting is muddled, both
muddleheaded and muddle-bodied, a preeminently
absurd activity in a world of absurdities. My shoulder
hit Etienne's midriff just as he groaned, not from the
blow but with release. He toppled sideways, tripping
on his trousers. Thereafter, I have a confused memory
of slapping and pushing and pulling and mistimed
attempts at punching and kicking, while he hopped
about cursing me, telling me to stop, lashing out with
one arm and trying to pull up his trousers with the
other hand. To be honest, I once witnessed a fight
between a couple of pubescent girls who were better
at it than Etienne and me. Physical strength, mascu-
line traits are not enough except in so far as they dis-
pose us toward an uncommon degree of imbecility. Or
maybe it was just because we were "men of science."
We didn't have the knack of it. We were like a pair of
warring windmills, sails spinning wildly to little purpose other than wearing down the internal works. At
length, he got a grip on the waistband of his breeches
and managed to tie a rough knot in the drawstring.

We were standing face-to-face, breathing heavily and sweating in the hot night air.

"What do you think you're doing, you idiot?"

He seemed genuinely perplexed.

"And you?" I said. "What were you doing? To her."

Marie-Jeanne was breathing heavily, too, but had yet to cover herself. A snail trail of semen was smeared across her thigh.

"I would have thought it was fairly obvious what I was doing. Are you mad?"

"Maybe, but not because of what I did there. Mad to have placed any confidence in a man like you perhaps."

"I wouldn't worry, there's plenty to go around. She's very free with her favors."

I took a step toward him, a step that was menacing enough for him to grasp the nearest weapon that came to hand, which happened to be a wooden hay fork.

"Stand back," he said, brandishing the fork.

"That was rape!" I screamed.

Marie-Jeanne shushed me.

"Quiet, don't wake my brother and father."

"You see," said Etienne. "The girl doesn't want it known."

"Because they'd kill you," she said, finally smoothing down her skirts and bending to recover her clogs, which had slipped off in the struggle.

"I'll kill you myself," I said.

"Don't be childish," said Etienne.

"Do you feel no shame?"

"I don't go in for shame," he said. "Regrets, yes. Which, until you so rudely interrupted, I was remedying as you advised."

This was too much for me. I lunged at him again, regardless of the hay fork. Fortunately the wood was old and brittle. The tines snapped as Etienne thrust the prong at my chest. I brushed aside the shaft and seized him by the neck of his shirt. Etienne seized me back and we began a lumbering dance, shaking one another as if we were each wielding a winnowing shovel, heads billowing back and forth like bags of chaff, which in truth they were. Eventually Etienne broke my grip by abruptly knocking both arms aside, then shoved me hard, causing me to stumble back and tumble over the beam of an old plow.

"Enough," he cried, as I got back on my feet. "Stop this nonsense. If you would squabble over a mere girl, you are more fool than I thought."

"Glad to be a fool if the term comes from a man who would force himself on a woman."

"I forced myself on nobody," he said, picking up his waistcoat. "Rape is physically impossible. Every man knows that. Shake a scabbard and you'll never get a sword in it."

"You were holding her down."

"All part of the game," he said, fastidiously dusting muck and threads of straw from the garment. "Let her deny it. She doesn't know her own self. Even if consent is tacit, it is there."

"You are a scoundrel. A heinous, despicable man without honor."

"You will not impugn my honor!"

"You impugn it yourself. A miscreant, a maggot, a man, I repeat, without honor."

"You will withdraw those words."

"I will not."

"Then I will have satisfaction."

"That is a challenge?"

"It is."

"Accepted."

—⁓—

"I forbid it. You will not do this stupid thing on my account."

"I have my honor too."

"You'll have nothing at all when he puts a bullet through your brain."

Etienne had gone, leaving Marie-Jeanne and myself to a conversation that was proving more awkward than I would have predicted. She was grateful for my intervention, but she was also in a white-hot fury, incensed at how it had turned out. She had rallied remarkably well after her ordeal, though I had no idea how she felt inside herself. People have had to accustom themselves to all manner of monstrous behaviors and women rather more than most, but I don't suppose it makes it any easier knowing such trials are the common lot of your sex. And it probably doesn't help having some pompous dunderhead prating about his honor. I hope I made it up to her afterward. I think I did. But she was in no mood for having things made up to her that night. She concluded her statement about putting a bullet through my brain by muttering, "If he can find it."

She had never reached the goats. Knowing her habits, Etienne had been waiting for her at the near end of the barn and had surprised her before she approached the livestock. Had she done so, the commotion they raised might have alerted us in time. She now continued down to the pens at the far end of the building while I trailed behind her.

"What he said. You know. I mean, about scabbards and swords. I don't believe it."

"Plenty will," she said. "Which is why you will not speak of it."

"Even to your family?"

"Especially to them. Because they won't believe it and they'll be after his blood."

"But why didn't you cry out?"

"You think I wanted it, like he said?"

"No, of course not. I didn't mean that. But if . . . I don't know. We might have come sooner."

"You didn't hear what I said back there? You weren't listening? To me, I mean, not to yourself. I will not have my father and brother charged with murder for me. Do you understand? And I will not have you die for me. You must put an end to this foolishness. Go to him, apologize, do whatever it takes."

"I'm afraid I can't do that."

She stopped then, turned to face me. We were in front of the stall where Molly was stabled.

"Why? It is a simple matter."

"A simple matter that is beyond my wit. I told you, I have my honor too."

"Well you are right in one thing, at least. You are lacking in wit. Honor is a fancy invented by men who have no proper respect for life or themselves or anyone else. It's a stupid code to make up for something they lack inside themselves. If you understand the reality of people, you don't need to make a shield for yourself like honor. Especially not one that can only be proved by killing. Do you know anything about guns?"

She had me there.

"No," I said, "but Molly does."

"Idiot."

She had me there too.

THE ATMOSPHERE in the Cazalets' household the next day
was fraught. Marie-Jeanne was still furious, a fury
that intensified when I ignored her repeated demands
to call the whole thing off. Looking back at it, I find
my intransigence puzzling, but there was a willful
stubbornness to my insistence that I had committed
myself and could not withdraw. I discovered later that
she even went to Etienne with the intention of begging
him to desist, but he wouldn't receive her. That she
was, for my sake, prepared to abase herself in front of
the man who had violated her perhaps explains what
happened after the duel.

Berenguer, meanwhile, was suspicious. He kept
asking what it was really all about.

"You're not going to fight a duel because you quarreled over the affections of a girl," he said, this being
the story I had let him understand, without specify-
ing it in so many words. "Marie-Jeanne is free to do
what she wants, you know. Leave her choose whoever
she wants. And if she wants neither of you, so be it.
Nobody's going to win her by killing somebody else, I
can tell you that much. I know my daughter."

The way he looked at me, it was plain he thought
I had taken leave of my senses and could not possibly
be the man he had imagined. I was sorry to disappoint
him, for I was genuinely fond of him, but I'd probably
be dead within the day, so it didn't really matter what
he thought of me. That I would die was clearly the
most likely outcome. As I said earlier, I knew nothing
about firearms, but a man of Etienne's class would
have more than a passing idea of how to get a bullet
from gun to target.

Marie-Jeanne's anger and Berenguer's disappointment notwithstanding, I had found one friend, and
that in a most unexpected quarter. As soon as he

heard what was to happen, Ramond offered to act as my second and had parlayed with Citizen Dalbaret who, somewhat surprisingly, had been appointed Etienne's representative. Neither party being prepared to apologize, the duel was set for the early hours of the following morning. Indeed Ramond had done more than act as a mere intermediary, for he had lent me his pistol and shown me how the thing worked. This had only exacerbated Marie-Jeanne's exasperation, for it now had a second incentive, and her humor was so incendiary that the heat she gave off might have baked an egg. Having left both of us in no uncertainty about her feelings, she was refusing to talk to us, and when obliged to communicate, did so through the agency of her father, even when we were in the same room together. It was all, "Tell my brother this" and "Inform our guest that."

Ramond's motives were obscure. He displayed none of Berenguer's incredulity and did not ask for details of the quarrel that had occasioned the duel. He could, of course, simply have been happy that at least one unwelcome intruder was likely to be removed from the scene. That thought did cross my mind. It may even have been in his mind, in some hidden corner he didn't care to explore. Marie-Jeanne certainly thought so. But I believe there was something else there too. The way he behaved toward me on what was supposed to be my last day was candid, the friendliness unfeigned as best I could determine. That afternoon, he even showed me one of the books he was smuggling into Spain.

The paper was poor quality, the binding not likely to last long either, but posterity was not the purpose. The book was an anthology of enlightened thought, or better enlightened passions. I had rarely read

Spanish, but I knew enough to see that the compendium opened with translations of Voltaire's shorter texts, among them, the *Petite Digression* and *Le Taureau Blanc*. There were selections from Rousseau, too, but the true nature of the work was disclosed by the inclusion of extracts from Diderot's *Les Bijoux Indiscrets*. The talking genitals of that mischievous romance were followed by passages from *La Fille de Joie*, after which the volume closed with salacious illustrations (the captions were nothing but brief excerpts) of older works like *L'École des Filles, L'Académie des Dames, Vénus dans le Cloître,* and the *Mémoires de Saturnin*. The pictures made me feel quite dizzy. Some of the male members must have had an armful of blood in them while the improbably gymnastic pairing of organs made my own experiences appear virginal.

"You don't think this is in poor taste in the circumstances?" I asked.

"The circumstances?" said Ramond. I had forgotten he didn't know. But he did not seem inclined to know either, for he continued: "It's just what sells."

"Anticlerical texts and pornography?"

"They don't have the same freedoms in Spain," he said. "Like you didn't have the same freedoms in the rest of France we had here. We've got our customs, our habits. The new laws look like to violate them. In the meantime, I make a little money violating other people's laws."

The threat of change doubtless explained his previous hostility. Yet now Ramond was my ally and the only Cazalet who was really sanguine about the morning's agenda.

My own feelings were mixed. I can't say I relished the coming encounter, which I knew I was likely to lose, but I was curiously calm, as if it was out of my hands and I just had to turn up at the appointed hour to let events take their course, events whose outcome I was in no way able to influence. Even when Ramond proposed practicing firing the gun, I said it didn't much matter, as I would not improve nonexistent skills in the time available. This probably wasn't true, but I was discovering a fatalistic streak in my character of which I had been previously unaware. The discoveries I made during the duel were even more revealing.

———

As I'd understood it, we were meeting at dawn in a remote valley to conduct business away from prying eyes. If that was the intention, it was a forlorn hope. There are no secrets in a small community like Tauzet and more people had turned out to witness the duel than attended my display of triangulation. They were lined along the slopes on either side of the valley. Nobody spoke, but the silence sounded loud with anticipation.

"They've come to see me killed," I said.

"More have come to see Vidal killed," said Ramond. "But you'll do as well. Courage, man. We'll see their priorities fulfilled yet."

I did not share his confidence. I'm not sure he did either. He looked pretty grim.

Etienne and the factor were already at the far end of the valley. Etienne was glowering at the crowd, their impertinent presence overcoming even his inveterate good humor. Ramond told me to wait where I was while he discussed the final arrangements with Dalbaret. Scanning the spectators' faces, I was relieved to see that neither Marie-Jeanne nor Berenguer were there. We had left before first light when neither of them were in evidence. Given the likely outcome, it was as well anyone who had felt some affection for me did not witness the event. When Ramond returned he was looking even grimmer than before.

"You look like you're the one about to die," I said.

"My intention is that nobody dies," he said.

"I'm not sure that's how these things work," I said.

"Oh, it is. The rules are made to avoid fatalities."

The onlookers weren't going to be pleased. If they were happy to see either party die, both would be better. There would be a gratifying symmetry to it. Avoiding fatalities was neither here nor there. People do have the most peculiar tastes. There is something unmapped in the human heart, a dark continent that is home to our most morbid desires, and even the greatest poets only seem able to sketch the edges of this terrain's dismal topography. Perhaps it is as well. If we really understood it, we could not live with ourselves.

"The purpose of a duel," said Ramond, "is to satisfy honor. Death is incidental and generally undesirable."

"I had no idea," I said.

"No," he said, looking at me obliquely. "Marie-Jeanne said as much."

I wasn't sure how to take this.

"You are certain you don't want to apologize?" he asked. I tutted my reproof. "No, I imagined not, but I have to ask. All right, in theory the duel is not *à l'outrance.*"

"Isn't it an excessive business anyway?"

"*Outrance* is the term for a duel fought to the death. The insult here is so obscure that nobody could pretend satisfaction demands a death. However, Vidal is not prepared to desist after first blood. He wants to continue until one of you is incapacitated."

There was more to dueling than just standing there blasting away at one another, which was more or less what I had been expecting. Apparently there were degrees of trying to kill each other, or salvaging honor, or whatever it was we were doing. I was faintly annoyed by all the formalities. I would have preferred to just get on with it and have done with the affair.

"You do appreciate the dangers," said Ramond. "Such a premise means death is still possible. It's not too late to make your excuses."

"I'm not here to keep myself safe, you know."

I was not being frivolous, not merely, at least. But these precautions and hedging about the issue struck me as hypocritical. We were going to point guns at each other and endeavor to insert small balls of metal into the soft bits of our counterpart's body, and all the bits of a body are soft when brought into contact with a quickly moving bullet. Dressing it up with protocol wasn't going to change that.

"You won't be needing my pistol. Vidal has brought a brace of dueling pistols. They belonged to his father."

"Runs in the family, does it? That doesn't sound good."

"It makes no difference to you since you refused to practice with my pistol. But it does mean each party will be equally well-armed. We choose which pistol we use. Or, at least, I will if you have no objections. The seconds load and prime. All you have to do is aim, then pull the trigger. The agreed distance is thirty paces. Dalbaret and I shall walk them out first, then mark the length by driving sticks into the ground. You and Vidal take up position at your respective sticks."

The ritual put me in mind of mapping a terrain. The rules were like precepts prescribing the proper way to proceed, except in this case the process was without purpose or meaning. That was why it required such an elaborate code. Otherwise it would collapse because there was nothing substantial to sustain it. It all felt a little unreal.

"You understand?" said Ramond.

"What? Oh, yes, sticks in the ground."

"You and Vidal take up position at your respective sticks."

"And start banging away at one another?"

"No, you start. The challenged fires first. Then if he's not seriously wounded, it's his turn."

"And we just carry on like that until one of us falls down?"

"You're not taking this seriously. And I doubt it will last that long. If it does . . . but, no, Vidal won't let that happen. He doesn't want to be humiliated. Too many shots make the duel seem absurd. He'll ensure you don't make him look ridiculous."

"Absurd, you say?"

This was something for a connoisseur.

—◦◦◦—

Standing at my post, I realized how appallingly close thirty paces can be. Perhaps that's the point. You don't want to be too distant when it's personal. You need to know you are about to kill someone. The green eyes were distinctly visible and I was seized by the deranged idea that I mustn't hit him in the face. Whatever else happened, I didn't want to destroy the perfection of those features. It was nonsense though. The life would soon seep out of the eyes if he got a bullet in the heart.

Despite the physical proximity, everything seemed slightly remote at the same time. The mind is marvelously devious and among the many tricks at its disposal is a capacity to wrap danger in a bubble of dreamlike unreality. Later, when we look back and the imagination gets to work, the dangers are terrifying, but at the time they are simply distant happenings to which we must respond. It's the brain's way of sidestepping paralyzing panic. In the circumstances, it is the least that erratic organ can do. Often as not it is the brain that gets the body into these predicaments in the first place.

I took one last look around the valley, drinking in the brimming light that was filling the hollows as the sun rose over the hills. The hush was intense. It seemed everybody had forgotten to breathe. The only sound was the faraway call of a hoopoe. I had always liked hoopoes. The *oop-oop* of the call from which they take their name sounds hopeful to me, an impression confirmed by their dipping, gravity-defying flight. They always look like they're about to pitch into the ground before flapping gaily away again, as if they keep forgetting to fly, then remember just in time to avert disaster. Yet the hoopoe has a bad reputation. I read somewhere that the unmannerly word for a woman of allegedly loose morals, *salope*, comes from *sale huppe*, the dirty hoopoe. And I believe in some cultures the call is considered an augury of death.

"Gentlemen, are you ready?" Ramond's voice brought me back to myself, but not before I realized that my surroundings were familiar. I hadn't recognized it before, but Marie-Jeanne and I had been here mapping. We had triangulated three monoliths defining the valley, one at the crux and two on the flanks. "I am duty bound to offer you each one last chance. If either of you would be willing to apologize . . ."

Dalabert snorted at this, earning himself a sharp glance of reprimand from Etienne. Snorting wasn't part of the protocol. But it betrayed Dalabert's motivation for acting as my opponent's second. What better way to revenge himself on the world than fomenting murder?

"Citizen Vidal?"

"I will not apologize," said Etienne.

"Citizen Darbon?"

"I have nothing to apologize for," I said. "At least not to that man."

Etienne colored, the first time I had seen him unsettled by words alone.

"Then the duel must proceed as planned and according to custom. Citizen Vidal offered the challenge, so Citizen Darbon has first shot."

Ramond and Dalabert met between us, the latter holding a wooden case carrying Etienne's guns. Ramond inspected the pistols closely before selecting one and preparing it. When he handed it to me, I was surprised how heavy it was. But then it is perhaps appropriate that a weapon of death should be heavy. There are some circumstances where lightness would be crass.

Etienne stood sideways, reducing my target. He needn't have bothered. He raised his chin, studying me with his glorious green eyes. I wished he had been a better man. I almost felt I was half in love with him. I don't know why, but maybe because he was all the things I was not: handsome, wealthy, privileged, educated, at ease in the world, a man who knew his past and was assured of his future.

"Present!" shouted Ramond.

We were certainly that.

The seconds withdrew to a safe distance.

I glanced at Ramond.

"At your will, Citizen Darbon," he said.

The moment had come. I raised my gun.

—⁓—

PHYSICAL COURAGE is a curious thing. I'm not particularly courageous morally or emotionally, but I discovered that day that I don't much mind dying. Appearances notwithstanding, I was in no hurry to embrace it. Nowadays, the matter is out of my hands. Death will take me soon enough. But I don't mind. My children will live on and my children's children, and on and on. Even if I had not had children, I would have found a similar solace in the sense of generations unfolding through the centuries, other people living their lives, making their discoveries, committing their crimes betimes, undoubtedly making their mistakes, hopefully learning from some of them. It is comforting to think of the world continuing without me. I knew it then, I know it now.

I raised the gun and leveled it on Etienne.

He did not flinch, but continued to gaze at me. He had his courage too.

I raised the gun and leveled it on Etienne; then raised it again, swiftly, so that it was pointing into the air, and pulled the trigger.

Several things happened at once. A woman screamed before the blast partially deafened me. The kick of the explosion jarred my shoulder painfully. And Etienne's face contorted. For a moment, I thought I'd managed to shoot him after all, but there was no blood and I realized the expression conveyed rage rather than pain. Then, as a newfound connoisseur of human absurdity, I had a brief moment of panic, wondering where the ball would land. It would be a fine comedy if I shot myself through the top of the head.

The ringing in my ears faded and before long I could hear a commotion coming from all sides. Several of the spectators were shouting, some were hooting and laughing, others chattering and debating, but the most strident voice belonged to Etienne, who was clearly livid.

"He deloped," he screamed. I had never seen him so indignant, even when I had tackled him in the barn. "You all saw it, he deloped. He is insulting me further. I will not have it. He cannot do that. It is a gross breach of etiquette."

He was waving his own gun so violently that I feared he might shoot some innocent bystander. Dalabert had the same idea, because he stepped smartly to one side so that he was well behind his principal.

"What's all the fuss about?" I asked, as Ramond approached.

"You're not meant to do that," he said. "Throw away your shot. It suggests your opponent is not worth killing. That he is unworthy of the field of honor. Even that he is not a gentleman."

"I thought it was rather gallant of me myself."

"Honor takes a different view."

I was beginning to see what Marie-Jeanne meant about honor.

It hadn't been planned. The decision to fire in the air had been taken at the last moment. I had never even heard of deloping in the context of a duel. But I must admit, there had been something instinctive in the gesture that was not mere dash. I did not want to kill Etienne. I did not want to kill anyone. But what Ramond had said about absurdity had struck a chord. I did not want to kill Etienne, but I did not in the least mind humiliating him. And humiliated he was. Something inside me must have intuitively known this would be the case. He was trembling all over, striding up and down behind his mark, calling upon all to witness my infamous behavior, insisting we proceed with a proper respect for the field of honor.

"It was a mistake," muttered Ramond.

"No, I did it on purpose," I said. "I admit, I hadn't anticipated it having quite such a dramatic impact."

"No, a strategic mistake. It will be his shot now."

"Very good," I said.

Ramond looked at me with his mouth open. There was something not far removed from admiration in his eyes.

"You are sure?" he said.

"I don't believe I have much choice in the matter," I said.

"You could forfeit your honor, walk away."

"Well, in that case, we had better get on with it then, hadn't we? Your shot, I believe, Citizen Vidal."

For a moment, I thought Etienne might explode with rage. If it hadn't been for the fact that I was about to die, I fancied I could get a taste for this.

—⁓—

IT WAS only afterward that I learned I had not even turned sideways to reduce the target. I faced Etienne chest forward. This was not bravado on my part, but negligence. Like so many things that have come to pass in my career, it was the result of oversight. This is strange for someone who espouses attentiveness as the principal tool in life, but when I speak of paying close attention, I mean to the outside world, for the external forms of the world are infinitely lovely, and in looking at them closely we realize ourselves far more fully than when we focus exclusively on ourselves and our personal well-being. The more you neglect yourself, the happier you will be, whatever Socrates has to say on the matter. Even the frightening things can be fascinating. Consequently, I won a wholly unmerited reputation for bravery.

Etienne squinted along the length of the barrel. The aperture of the muzzle was like a second eye, one quick and lively, the other dead and deadly. I could detect a very slight tremor in his hand. I thought this might be excitement, but Ramond insisted it was a result of Etienne's outrage, and that very likely it was my scandalous disregard for protocol that saved my life. Either way, the next few seconds seemed to elongate, every instant a well-defined moment in itself.

Etienne squeezed the trigger.

The hammer clicked forward.

The jaws struck the gun's frizzen.

There was a puff of smoke from the pan.

His hand jerked upward.

The report seemed to reach me several seconds later though it must have been less than that.

At first, I felt I must be failing to play the game properly again, for I had not fallen over and, insofar as I could determine, was not yet dead, which I imagined was what protocol expected of me. Had Etienne deloped? It didn't seem likely. He swallowed hard, blinked once, bit his lip. There was a gasp from the onlookers, a soft sound made loud by many voices. Ramond was at my side fingering my shoulder.

"Blood has been drawn," he announced.

Somebody had been shot? I was concerned one of the spectators had paid dear for their injudicious curiosity, but then I became aware of a burning sensation in my left shoulder. My shirt sleeve was torn at the top of the humerus and bright blood was soaking into the material.

"Citizen Vidal," said Ramond. "This is enough. Each of you has fired a shot. Honor is served. We may call a halt to the duel now."

"Can you move your arm, Citizen Darbon?" asked Etienne.

I made the experiment. It stung, but I was in no way handicapped, the movement was fluid. The bullet had not embedded itself, just grazed the flesh, incidentally ruining my one good shirt. Not that I'd be needing that much longer, but it seemed a pity to waste perfectly decent linen.

"Yes, thank you very much," I said.

No irony was intended, but my reply elicited laughs from the onlookers, and caused the light to dance in Etienne's eyes again.

"The duel is not done," he said, his voice clipped and peeved. "Your shot, Citizen Darbon."

Again the crowd was gasping. Being an innocent in these matters, I did not understand why, but I was later told a duel rarely took so long and the drama of such a protracted combat was rare. It seemed my first idea, that we just stood there banging away at one another until somebody fell down, was finally nearer the mark.

Ramond had left me to consult with Dalabert, who in turn went to Etienne. He said a few words, after which Etienne shook his head firmly.

"We continue," he said.

RAMOND RELOADED my pistol. I was growing weary of all this. The sun had risen high enough to heat the valley and I could feel sweat trickling from my armpits while the blood slowly advanced along the length of my sleeve.

"Aim true," said Etienne.

He did not turn sideways this time. Perhaps honor forbade it. I was still unaware of the fact that I had failed to turn, but in the way of these things I suppose once one party has displayed what is misinterpreted as suicidal bravery, the other must follow suit.

Fatigue and mounting irritation made me lax. Even a connoisseur of absurdity becomes bored with the world's insanity sometimes. I did not shoot into the air. I pointed the gun vaguely in Etienne's direction. I lowered the barrel a fraction. I still did not want to spoil those eyes. And I moved it slightly to the left.

"Aim true," he repeated.

I tensed the muscles in my arm. Having felt the impact of the skyward shot, I didn't want the gun jumping out of my hand or firing at the crowd. Even so, when I pulled the trigger, the recoil jolted my arm to the right.

The blast and the smoke blocked my perception of the outside world for an instant. When I could see clearly again, I almost wished I couldn't. Etienne was doubled over at the waist, his hands clasped to his midriff, blood staining his smart white breeches. This was not what I had wanted. Even I knew that a wound to the belly was generally fatal and always intensely painful. Then he straightened up. To my relief, he was not gut shot. The blood was coming from his hand, his right hand. The two forefingers were badly man-gled. One seemed to have disappeared altogether. His shattered gun was lying on the ground.

This time the gasping was promptly followed by clapping and cheering. I briefly thought I'd won some friends.

"The duel is finished!" cried Ramond, quick to extricate me from any further folly. "Citizen Darbon's shooting hand is incapacitated."

Even Etienne was not angry enough to try shooting with his left hand.

"I've made myself popular, I think," I said to Ramond.

His shoulders dropped.

"It's not you they're applauding," he said. "It's your marksmanship."

"My marksmanship? I just pointed the thing at random."

"They don't know that. They saw you purposefully throw away your first shot to avoid killing him. Then, when you were obliged to shoot at him, you carefully maimed his shooting hand to put an end to the duel without ending his life. They would have preferred another outcome, but they appreciate the skill that disappointed them."

The things people read into the world! But it gave me an idea.

"Citizens!" I shouted. "Please, listen to me. Here you see the potency of triangulation. I have mapped this valley. I know its every dimension. And because of this scientific precision, I was able to assess the exact angle at which I should aim my pistol. You see the many applications that can be made of this technology? You would do well to embrace them."

I was not really serious. It was just a bit of fun, no more than mischief. But the clapping stopped. Everyone was staring at me with stupefaction and wonderment. This was magic of a different order altogether.

Ballistics brought home. Maybe Etienne had helped my cause after all. The only person not overawed by my marvelous, supernatural skills was Marie-Jeanne. She was marching toward me, brushing aside anyone who had the temerity to get in her way.

—⁓—

SHE MARCHED right up to me. Didn't hesitate. Right up to me. Knew where she was going. Knew what she was doing too. Stopped right in front of me. And she drew back her arm. And she flattened her hand. And she swung her arm through what I reckon was an arc of near 107 degrees, though I wasn't calculating it at the time, and I never asked her to repeat the gesture in order to measure it accurately. I could see it coming. I wasn't that daft. But it seemed so improbable that I just stood there and watched her open palm curving toward me. Etienne's bullet hadn't been anything like as fascinating. I couldn't have been more confounded had it been the hand of God himself descending to smite some biblical miscreant. Except the hand was ascending and I didn't believe I was any manner of miscreant. Odd sort of god too.

She slapped me hard across the cheek.

"Don't you ever do that to me again," she said.

She was a bit cross.

"What?"

The blow had possessed considerably more force than any landed by Etienne and myself in the barn. It wasn't what I was expecting. Not much on the conquering hero front, if you know what I mean. I don't suppose Pompeia clouted Caesar about the head when he came home from giving Vercingetorix the once-over in Gaul.

"Do not do that to me ever again," she enunciated.

"You just slapped me. You did it to me."

"Not that. The anguish of fearing you were going to be killed. I will not stand for it."

I now know a bit more about how people work, notably women, and I know that they have some quaint ideas about the living and dying of their loved ones. As far as I can see it's all fairly straightforward: you've got to do the latter sooner or later, so best hope you've done a bit of the former first, and you won't do any living if you spend your time worrying about dying. But women don't always see it like that. They're set on keeping us alive.

"Are you listening?"

"I'm listening," I said, fingering my cheek, which was smarting rather more than my shoulder. Given the look in her eyes, listening seemed the wisest course of action.

"I will not have you behaving in such a stupid and reckless way. Is that understood?"

"Understood."

"Understood what?"

"Um . . . I don't know. Understood, sir?"

Her eyes widened with disbelief and her mouth dropped open. I had a talent for dumbfounding the Cazalets. I wondered whether she had assimilated the concept of human absurdity as wholeheartedly as I had. She made a movement. I braced myself for another blow. Apparently Marie-Jeanne adhered to the same pedagogical principles favored by my masters at the orphanage. But this time she didn't slap me. Instead she flung her arms around my neck, much like I had with Molly in the maze, and hung on tight in case I got lost again. I did not shy away.

Berenguer was standing behind his daughter. He was grinning, nodding, winking, and making furtive knowing gestures all at the same time.

"I told you she'd make her choice," he said.

Something sealed, some promise made, something confirmed.

It wasn't the most conventional declaration of love. But I could live with that.

—⁓—

WHEN LIFE is turned upside down, the underside often looks dingy, but when love does the turning, nothing dazzles like topsy-turvy. This is one of those fatuous truisms that bears repetition because everyone needs to confirm it through personal experience at least once in a lifetime and, if you haven't, you should be asking yourself why. In the following weeks, Marie-Jeanne and I enjoyed a betrothal honeymoon so blissful that it was almost brainless. That we were to wed was understood by all. Those arms looped about my neck were more binding than any ring. Tighter still was the knot tied by traipsing over the hills and mountains of Tauzet.

I had never been blind to Marie-Jeanne's beauty. It had hit me that first day when she descended the cliff. And her wit had whacked me harder still. But the yearning of young men is no measure of depth or durability. It was in the landscape that the bond had been made. Learning to love the land, I had been learning to love her, and by walking into the world together, we had unwittingly become a couple.

Even the driest disciplines possess a whisper of poetry and there is a lovely phrase in geodesy, "the attraction of mountains." Science deems it a defect, but the world does not defer to man-made conventions, and it has been proven that the mass of a mountain generates its own gravity that can deflect a plumb line and distort the readings of a theodolite, thus invalidating calculations of latitude and longitude. We literally no longer know where we are. But if you are open to the emotional distortions brought about by mountains, their attraction is altogether more beneficent. Rather than disorienting me, the mountains I explored with Marie-Jeanne had oriented me. I had found myself and my place in the world. The discovery reminded me of the epigraph to Jean Guillaume Garnier's *Traité d'Algèbre,* a citation from d'Alembert, "Come, sir, only begin and faith will follow." We don't need to understand everything immediately. If we admit unknowing and keep on exploring, understanding will come.

To celebrate our union, Marie-Jeanne and I made a new map, one we dubbed the Map of Love. It was childish, but we all retain something of the child inside us. Many people cling to poorly managed emotions, raging self-obsession, and a tendency to stamp their feet when life does not cooperate with their expectations. It would be better if we could cultivate the spontaneity, creativity, and naive love of the visible world that are given to us in youth, and which we often mislay in the process of erosion called growing up. My own childhood was marked by a misfortune that nearly stifled these things before I knew they existed, but I have seen them since, and I now understand that they were redeemed in me by Marie-Jeanne, with whom I worked my way back to an Eden I had not known before.

After copying onto a clean sheet the features we had previously surveyed, Marie-Jeanne and I proceeded to rename them, composing an emotional geography of moments and memories we cherished. Thus the *Saut de Procureur* turned into Goat Girl's Descent in honor of our first meeting. The Peak of Human Absurdity was the summit on which I had told her about my mishap in Vauriennes. The factor had caught me sketching her at Squint Rock. Lalande's strange appetites inspired Spider Grove, while the frictioners of the spa towns gave birth to Tummy Rubbers' Tree. The falls and her secret cave became The Pool of the Magic Triangle, a magic we measured precisely the next time we visited that sacred place. As for Slap Valley, I need hardly tell you where that was.

In naming these places, we made the landscape our own, making a kind of treasure map of the riches we had found together, so that we were in sort mapping ourselves. But we were not merely mapping our past together. We were also mapping our future, plotting the world we hoped to share for the rest of our days.

Once the new map was labeled, I began refining the relief hachures below Goat Girl's Descent, which had been drawn before Marie-Jeanne invented contour lines. But instead of simply representing the slope and crags, I incorporated Marie-Jeanne's portrait into the topography, inspired by the "Moon Maiden" hidden in the engraving of Cassini's *Carte de la Lune*. It was done on a whim, but it seemed fitting. As far as I was concerned, she was the mountain and the mountain was Marie-Jeanne. And I was in there, too, figuratively speaking, the maker who inadvertently but inevitably reveals himself in the thing he makes.

Geographical engineers maintain that by measuring and mapping a mountain they tame it, turning what was wild and intimidating into something tractable that they can possess. But it doesn't work like that. Mapping, sketching, telling stories, any creative work aspires to capturing a certain truth about its subject. But you never possess it. All you can do is evoke a partial reality that seems right to the reader. What is true, though, is that the creative process possesses you. A mountain is more than how high it is, but you can take the measure of a mapmaker from the maps he makes. Drawing the Map of Love taught me this.

Mapping plays curious tricks on us. Our most famous mapmakers are astronomers, for in studying the stars we study the earth. Like sailors taking a bearing at sea, we look elsewhere to see where we are. The night sky had been a distraction in Paris, an escape from painful confusion. Now mapping had brought me down to earth, rooting me in place and time. That's what I believed, at least, in those heady weeks after the duel. But another world was out there, a world not of our making, and it had other plans for Marie-Jeanne and me.

Disappointed by the outcome of a duel in which both parties had perversely declined to die, Dalabert arranged for Etienne to be transported to Limoux, where a surgeon could repair his shattered hand. The injuries were not life threatening and no infection had set in, so we had no need to fear a legal investigation. But Etienne was still the *Inspecteur des Eaux et Forêts*, he would be back to assess the damage done by goats in the woods, and he was still the representative of the departmental directorate, in which capacity he could do damage of his own.

The disorder resulting from the revolution was never far away, even if facts remained as elusive as ever. The most evident symptom was the porous border. It had never been hermetic, but bandits and smugglers were

becoming increasingly bold as the tussle for power
in Paris temporarily weakened central authority. We
heard, for instance, that a band of Spanish *miquelets*
had raided a village in the neighboring valley, killing
two men and a goat. And one night, we witnessed
a column of torches winding its way down from the
uplands. It was a caravan of smugglers, larger than
any we had seen before, their contraband protected by
a small army that could have tackled a company of
regular troops. Even Ramond, whose business was on
an infinitely smaller scale, felt compelled to escalate
his activities to profit from the precarious situation,
and went to Carcassonne to procure more banned
books.

Meanwhile, in the Cazalet household, we indulged
in a domestic triangulation, taking the measure of our
transformed relations. Berenguer was cock-a-hoop,
claimed he had known for weeks what was coming,
promised to pay off the inevitable *charivari* himself,
and praised the Map of Love as a pledge for the future
of his family. He was so taken by the map that he even
boasted in the village about Marie-Jeanne's new portrait, which was not the wisest thing to do. The Cazalets understood that my idle jest about triangulating
the dueling ground had been a joke. But when I happened upon other locals, I sensed that my status as
arch necromancer had been heightened by the claim.
Some displayed a grudging respect, but most hurried
by, fearing further demonstrations of my thaumatur-
gical prowess. I was the man who could shoot off your
finger with a map. What they would make of my loved
one becoming a mountain was anybody's guess.

Nevertheless our lives remained serene for several
weeks as summer waned and autumn crept down
the mountain, the cooler mornings and shorter days

crimping the leaves on the trees. It was time for the shepherds to return from the high pasture and it was at the transhumance festival that everything fell apart again.

———〜〜———

THE TRANQUIL countryside had become a cacophony of bleating, lowing, barking, nickering, and, above all, jangling, the sheep, cattle, and horses jingling enough bells to quell Notre-Dame and the Vatican combined. The shepherds were big, burly, wild-looking men wearing frieze cloaks, wool caps, and forbidding faces. They were armed with thick staffs, short daggers, long carbines, and stranglers' hands, and comported themselves in a manner that suggested the wolves and bears would have been well-advised to swear off meat-eating for the duration.

For several days before the fair, a stream of outsiders had been arriving on foot, horseback, and perched on top of heavily laden carts. Cheese merchants and livestock dealers came first, followed by hucksters, bagmen, bohemians, mountebanks, and quacksalvers. A parallel community sprouted about Tauzet, peopled by tinkers, tallymen, cobblers, bodgers, quilters, hosiers, haymongers, chapmen, colporteurs, cardmakers, leeches, apothecaries, spooners, ropers, cutlers, tapsters, and itinerant brandy burners. There were showmen, too, bear leaders, acrobats, jugglers, fortune tellers, puppeteers, cup and ball conjurers, and traveling players promising "all the latest boulevard melodramas from Paris and the world."

The chaos was near complete and any ingredient that might have been missing from the ferment got mixed in when evening came and the dedicated

carousing began. I stayed well clear of the shepherds.
They looked scary enough without the addition of
a six-month thirst and a skinful of moonshine that
could scour copper. The delicate steps of the danc-
ing bears suggested an altogether more conspicuous
degree of gentility.

The air was thick with smoke from spit-roasts and
sizzling griddles. There were shouts and cries of uncertain sentiment, celebration sounding suspiciously like
murder, while musicians committed their own clamor-
ous murders, competing with one another to draw a
crowd that might pay a *sous* to dance. Flute and drum
duos accompanied *farandoles*, flame jumpers vaulted
through bonfires urged on by frenetic fiddle playing,
slide trumpets and tambourines inspired pirouettes
and leaps, young men swinging their partners high so
that skirts billowed wide revealing everything under-
neath. It was an education. Marie-Jeanne nudged my
elbow, reminding me I was all but a married man. I
grinned, shrugged, she laughed. Monsieur Le Curé,
meanwhile, was spitting fury at the scandalous spectacle and taking care to peek beneath the skirts the
better to stoke his outrage. The furnace was burning
strongly.

Everything was helter-skelter, harum-scarum, hugger-
mugger, higgledy-piggledy, hurly-burly, and the normally reserved country people seemed ready for any
madcap antic. To lure custom, one luckless quack
staged a bawdy play on the back of his cart featuring
a buxom maid carried off by a rapacious bear, not a
real one but a boy wearing a goatskin cloak and a
wobbly headdress. The lack of verisimilitude notwithstanding, the spectators were so provoked that they
took to the stage, laying about the youth with sticks
and clubs, and smashing for good measure the vials

containing the quack's nostrum. Their credulity in the face of such an improbable farce spoke volumes for the potency of my mapping.

"These people are crazy," I exclaimed, linking arms with Marie-Jeanne and reeling away from the teeming mob, who seemed inclined to castrate the "bear."

"I told you," said Marie-Jeanne. "Individuals don't count. Everything you feel, everything you want has to be held down, put aside. Like it's not there, not what you want. Today and carnival are the only times they can break loose."

She had broken loose, at least, asserting herself against the will of her neighbors. It showed too. You could see it in her eyes and the cast of her features. There was something inside her these days, something personal but not peculiar to herself, as if she were enhanced by a supplementary element. Captivated by love, I took that element to be me. Now we were made to serve one another, it seemed right that each should inhabit the other. I was mistaken, of course. I often am. No matter. It was a pardonable spasm of ego on my part.

"Yes, but they're meant to be happy today," I said. "What are they like when they're angry? This *chari-vari* we have to go through, what's that going to be? I thought it was just a bit of banging on a few pots and pans. Do you think we ought to rescue that bear?"

"That's the most of it, yes, the orchestra. And you pay a ransom, mainly in drink. And submit to the *asoade*."

"What's that?" Where these people were concerned, words I didn't understand worried me. "I really think that bear needs help."

"They're just funning him."

"Fun? It doesn't look much like fun to me. Look, they're taking his trousers off! What's an *asoade*? Is that fun, too?"

"Running the donkey," she said. "It's not so bad. We sit on the back of a donkey, me facing forward, you facing backward. And you hold the donkey's tail."

"I could do that," I said. "Do I get to keep my trousers on?"

"And everybody boos and jeers at us."

"Then we get married and live happily ever after?"

"We get married. The rest is up to us."

"And the donkey? Does he live happily ever after?"

But she never got to answer that, for it was then that we met Etienne.

———

HE WAS the worse for drink. I'd like to say he was the better for it, but it's true what Marie-Jeanne said, most men are less likable when in drink. The dark bits they keep to themselves tend to creep out for an airing. On the occasion when we had got drunk together, Etienne had become louder and increasingly excited about the revolution, but I was in such a deleterious state myself that I scarcely noticed what he revealed of himself. I probably told him I loved him too. But I didn't love the flushed figure who stumbled out of the crowd that evening. No, stumbled is putting it too strong. He was master of himself, still. But there was an air of unsteadiness about his movements and his eyes were not quite focused.

"Ah, the young lovers," he said, affably enough in the circumstances.

Marie-Jeanne said nothing.

"Good evening," I said, my voice wooden even to my own ears. "Your hand is . . . the wound, I mean. It is mending?"

He still wore a thick bandage, but it was clear that at least part if not all the forefinger was missing. He inspected the bandaged hand distantly, as if it was nothing to do with him.

"A pity," he said, at length. "I was very attached to that finger."

It was a good joke, but the maniacal laughter with which he greeted his own witticism purged it of any humor.

"I regret . . ."

"But I have a clerk," he said, interrupting my attempt at an apology.

"A clerk?"

"For writing, don't you know? It has been concluded. An offensive is required."

He looked from one to the other of us, like a quizzical bird.

"An offensive?" I said.

"Yes, against goats. My man and I shall be visiting you tomorrow. He has a neat hand. Very good for noting how many goats each household possesses and how many it should contribute to the cull. What do you think your share should be?"

I could feel Marie-Jeanne stiffen on my arm, but she still would not speak, this direct threat to her beloved herd notwithstanding. I noticed several people pointing at us. Despite the revels and the many strangers who knew nothing of what had happened, the meeting of two duelists was still worth watching.

"You should not let what has happened between us influence your professional duties," I said, trying to ignore the onlookers and remain calm, though I was far from calm inside. It's not every day you have a chat with a man who has tried to kill you, still less one you have maimed.

"What happened between us? I don't understand. But I can assure you, I don't let anything come between me and my work. I don't let anything come between me and anything. As you should well know."

He raised his undamaged hand, joined the tips of the middle finger and the thumb to form a circle, then jigged it from side to side. I could feel my cheeks burning. Marie-Jeanne's grip tightened on my arm.

"We were saying though," he continued, letting his hand drop. "The war on goats. I am perfectly serious. This is official business. The goats are a menace. At least one fifth must go. And I am to make the selection. I shall be at your farm tomorrow."

"You'll get no welcome," muttered Marie-Jeanne.

It was only the second time I had heard her say a word to him. And it was the last.

"Ah, she speaks. Do not worry. I expect no welcome. It is not in the nature of my job to be welcomed. And, as you know, I can take what I need when hospitality is wanting."

"You will desist from these allusions to . . ."

"I will desist from nothing," he replied hotly, cutting me off before I could finish. "The commission for the preservation of the nation's forests has entrusted me with a task and I will fulfill it as I see fit."

"I wasn't talking about that."

"I know what you were talking about, you guttersnipe. I have made inquiries about you, Citizen Darbon. And to think that I believed you had the makings of a gentleman. I am only glad I dipped mine before you. I would not have wanted to soil myself in a sheath . . ."

I broke from Marie-Jeanne's grip and shoved him hard in the chest. All eyes were on us now, but it was too late for discretion. He had his fingers circled again, wagging the hand back and forth, an insufferable little smile on his face.

"How's the scabbard? I trust you find it as steady as I did."

Marie-Jeanne skipped between us, grasping my shirtfront to hold me back. In the absence of anyone other than me being willing to lay hands on him, Etienne restrained himself, albeit at the same time conveying an urgent desire to throttle me. I can see it still, two strutting cocks, fluffing their feathers, puffing their chests, and raising their heads, ready to flutter up and bury their spurs in one another. Being a connoisseur carries a heavy burden sometimes.

"The nature of a rape is so very perplexed, and the perpetration of it on an adult person so very difficult, that it requires something of an implicit belief to be credited," said Etienne. "That is the legal view, you understand. If a woman puts up a sufficiently determined defense she cannot be violated. Any modest and decent woman worth her reputation will resist. Rape does not exist. Coitus is, by definition, reciprocal."

The hand was wiggling again, but he had been a little too explicit for his own good. Berenguer loomed out of the darkness and swung a rather lovely punch that caught Etienne on the side of the head. No shilly-shallying, either, he was straight in there. Once they put their mind to it, the Cazalets are very capable pugilists. I was full of admiration and was glad that good old man was going to be my father-in-law, but Marie-Jeanne didn't see the beauty of the gesture at all. She began giving her father a verbal dressing down that must have stung quite as much as the slap that sealed our engagement.

"That will cost you," shouted Etienne, holding the side of his head. "The fine for fighting is 450 *sous*."

"I can live with that," said Berenguer.

I half wondered if I could pay a fine myself and have a crack at him too. Then Citizen Pellaprat arrived with three militiamen. Marie-Jeanne was still castigating her father, her tongue sharp enough to calm him down considerably, while I was unwilling to break from her grip a second time, and Etienne clearly deemed us unworthy of physical contact, so the confrontation ended there. But I did make a point of embracing Berenguer and expressing my appreciation. The old man had wielded a most elegant fist, nicely judged, and nimbly delivered. Marie-Jeanne was incandescent. She was right to be angry too. I regretted my cocksure belligerence the next day when word came that Etienne's body had been found. He had been bludgeoned to death.

—◦◦◦—

DESPITE WHAT he did to Marie-Jeanne, I never hated Etienne. I did regret that his erudition and manners could mask a heart that regarded others as fodder for his appetites. Above all, though, he made me question myself. I had come to associate Etienne with all the things I wanted to be: educated, urbane, of the modern world, a man of science. Yet if their epitome was so corrupt, what did that say about those ambitions? I was not, even then, so dim as to damn an ideal for the failings of one man. But there was nonetheless a niggling feeling that, if he could be so wrong, maybe those things were not so right.

It was Ramond who brought us word of the murder. He returned from his book-buying expedition the following morning. The body had been found in a shallow gully not far from the fairground. The head had been bashed in with a blunt instrument. Nothing had been taken as far as Citizen Pellaprat could ascertain, so it did not seem to be the consequence of a casual robbery. Somebody had killed Etienne for personal reasons.

We sat at the kitchen table, as we had so many times before, but there was nothing festive about the mood. We all understood what this meant. No local would grieve for Etienne, but he was a government man going about government business. The death could not be ignored. The mayor had already sent for the magistrate. The culprit had to be caught. And it didn't take an Aristotle to deduce who would be the principal suspects.

I had fought a duel with Etienne. We had quarreled the previous evening. Berenguer had thumped him. The compromising of Marie-Jeanne had been proclaimed. Her violator was due to cull the family livestock. And Ramond had nobody to attest to his whereabouts, having been on the road all night. Any number of people might have done it. Foresters, herdsmen, Vidal's tenants, the lawless itinerants, *miquelets*, one of those terrifying shepherds. Any number of people had the means. Any number of people had the motive. But ours was declared.

"What are we going to do?" said Berenguer.

Neither of his children seemed to have any idea, so I spoke up.

"I shall draw a map," I said.

They looked at me like I had taken leave of my senses—again.

"A map?" said Ramond.

"Yes, a map."

"You don't think the situation calls for something a little more practical than that?"

I had the impression he half regretted leading me out of that maze.

"Nothing more practical than a map," I said. "I shall draw a murder map."

"Why?" said Marie-Jeanne, ever direct.

"You've all seen how they regard my work. The people of Tauzet, I mean. Even that first portrait. They're so superstitious, they fear people can be caught or multiplied by a pencil. That's the best argument there is for a pencil. It can draw out a truth. Well, that's what I aim to do. It's the same with the triangulating and the mapping. They see it as some sort of sinister magic. They even believed what I said when I shot Etienne. Imagine what they'll think when I tell them I am going to draw a map of the murder."

"They'll think you're a lunatic," said Ramond.

"So much the better. It will worry them even more."

"We don't have enough troubles without frightening the neighbors?" said Berenguer.

"But what is the purpose of this?" said Marie-Jeanne. I suspect she knew already.

"The Murder Map will include all the known details. I shall mark where the body was found, where Etienne went during the evening, what he did. Who saw what, said what, heard what, where they all were. It can be dressed up with estimated hours, calibrated with values copied from the logarithmic tables. Mathematical notation in the margins. Some Latin might help, a bit of Greek too. And the angles at all the points will be measured and key sites will be triangulated with the nearest dwellings. There must be as many measurements as possible, as many baffling details, the better to play up the magic of it."

"So?" said Ramond. "Like she said, why?"

"To find out who the murderer is."

"You can find a murderer by mapping the crime?"

"No, of course I can't. But while the magic holds, if people believe I can, if the story we're telling them seems plausible, it's as good as real. If I can shoot a man through mapping, I can track down a killer through mapping. It's just a question of creating a sufficiently compelling narrative. Sooner or later, whoever did this will become so scared, they will reveal themselves one way or another."

"There is a problem here," said Marie-Jeanne.

"There are lots of problems," I said. "We are fashioning an illusion. Illusions are always complicated."

"But there is one big problem. One very big problem. How do you think this killer is going to reveal himself?"

"I don't know. I hadn't thought of that. Run away? Confess?"

"Or try to stop the person who is about to expose him. Stop the person forever, I mean."

"That is a risk I shall have to take. Unless anyone has a better idea."

—◦◦◦—

Marie-Jeanne and I began work the next day while Berenguer and Ramond spread the word. First, though, I went to Citizen Pellaprat and asked to see the body. The mayor clearly found my request questionable, but acceded nonetheless, doubtless out of curiosity as much as any sense of civic duty. Etienne's remains were being kept in Citizen Gabadou's cellar until the magistrate arrived. Whoever killed him had certainly held a grudge. There was no light in those lovely eyes now and the back of his skull was such a mess that it hurt just to look at it. He was lying on his back, so his posture hid the worst damage, but the occiput was unnaturally flat, and gore matted his hair.

Contemplating the corpse, I had the strangest feeling I was looking at an elder brother, counterpart to myself, a kind of Cain who had had it all, possessing the rights and privileges of the first born, the power to have and to hold, the ownership of everything civilized. Yet he was the one who had been slain. I was the survivor, the son favored by fortune, the nomad come home. The world really was being turned on its head.

I may have been looking a little too closely, perhaps even murmuring to myself, because after a while I realized that I was being inspected in turn. Citizen Pellaprat was staring at me and there was nothing amiable in his look.

"He was my friend," I said, surprising myself as much as him with the statement.

"If you say so," he said, evidently disbelieving.

You may question it yourself. I am aware that my portrayal of Etienne in these pages has been almost entirely negative. I have written what took place in Tauzet at that time, but I don't doubt there was more to him than I have described. Judging by my infatuation, I intuited as much even then. I wasn't merely enchanted by his seductive intellect and beautiful green eyes. He was someone I would have liked to be in another life, not because he was privileged and knew how to take what he wanted of the world, but because he was of the world and of his times. I am not. My emotional dislocation in Paris was a precursor to the political and temporal dislocation in which I would spend the greater part of my life. I do not regret this. I cannot imagine a better life for the man I am than the one I have lived and I have engaged with the world in my own way. But I can imagine other ways of living and other ways of being. Sometimes I even wish I had the time and talent to explore them.

"I will find his killer," I said.

"The magistrate will do that," said the mayor.

His scrutiny suggested the magistrate would have more than a little prompting about where to look, confirming my conviction that the Murder Map was our only hope.

WE BEGAN at the scene of the crime. There were still many people camped out after the fair and I made a great show of measuring the gully with a length of rope borrowed from Berenguer. I took elaborate and totally meaningless sightings with the theodolite and quadrant, "confirmed" them with the circumferentor, had Marie-Jeanne act as rodman for further measurements, paced out the distances, walked them again with the perambulator, every act as ostentatious and as ostensibly laborious as I could make it.

And it worked. I don't mean it produced anything substantive. Guilty assassins weren't queuing up to receive absolution from the mathematical necromancer. But bystanders came to look and soon the locals emerged from their houses to follow my every move with cold, curious eyes. Once they were there, observed by their neighbors, I asked them questions, the where, when, who of it all, questions they felt constrained to answer because everybody was watching them and

anyone who didn't cooperate would be under suspicion. I noted it all down, every word of it, responding
to their answers with little exclamations, punctuat-
ing their testimonies with *Mmms* and *Hm-hmms* and
I-sees and, once in a while, a *Now-that's-interesting.*
I discovered that, judiciously used, a *Now-that's-
interesting* can cause no end of alarm. If ever anyone
were to make a profession of decrypting the human
mind, I would recommend it wholeheartedly. People
are always worried what they have betrayed when you
tell them it was interesting. It's like telling them they
are being brave.

I triangulated households in relation to the gully,
made ridiculous little parades of my ancient barometer, as if the emotional atmosphere might modify air
pressure. It was the purest flimflam and might even
have been amusing had the purpose not been so serious. But I could see it was having an impact, because
people closed their doors when I drew near, only opening them when I started telling the world at large
that there was a suspicious absence in this particular domicile. I even employed my plain table alidade,
though it was useless for any meaningful measurement, but it was one more tool, and its crooked form
matched my cockeyed purposes. I was trying to compute something invisible, something hidden round the
corner, and a bent instrument was the ideal device to
do it.

Naturally there was no guarantee the spectacle
would have the sought-after result. If the killer was
one of the itinerants, the task was hopeless, for the
showmen, hawkers, and merchants were breaking
camp and making for their next marketplace. Once
gone, they would be beyond my reach, no matter how
superstitious they were. But some instinct told me

Etienne's murderer was local, one of us, someone who knew him and what he was doing.

The first night, I sewed four sheets of paper together to make my Murder Map as imposing and intimidating as possible, then charted the details I had noted during the day, adding a few more of my own invention by way of embellishment. The next morning, I pinned the draft to the church door and, using a stick as a pointer, began explaining its intricacies to passers-by. It was most gratifying. Even as a work in progress, the map was compelling, and the more I elaborated, the more people happened to "pass by." My complacence was short-lived however.

The magistrate arrived.

I had a warm moment there.

———

PIERRE GASPARD was a small man of middle years with a large nose and a sharp eye. When he rode into the church square with half a dozen militiamen, my audience miraculously melted away, as if he were no mean magician himself. I was midway through my exposition though, so I persisted, reasoning that it would look suspicious if I packed up the instant he appeared. In the circumstances, I did not want to look suspicious in front of this man. He dismounted and watched my performance for a few minutes, then took me by the arm, and marched me into the church.

"What are you doing, you charlatan!" he said. "The fair is finished, the humbugs have moved on. This has nothing to do with mapping. It's just storytelling."

I could tell him something about that, but reckoned the moment wasn't propitious.

"You are a surveyor?" I asked, neutrally, while I collected my thoughts.

"An amateur astronomer. Sufficiently familiar with these instruments and the techniques of mapping to know you are talking nonsense."

There was no point dissembling. I told him everything, why I was there, how I had been received, my conflict with Etienne, even that I was his principal suspect. Somebody would inform him soon enough anyway. Thus the first confession elicited by the Murder Map was my own. It's funny how fictions work. You aim to expose somebody else and end up babbling about yourself.

He looked at me for a long time when I had finished. I don't know whether it was my temerity or that he simply liked the ruse I had outlined, but after a while he laughed, said I could continue with my experiment, but should report to him each day. He would be watching me.

"You are a determined and resourceful young man, at least," he said. "Continuing your work when your superiors have been obliged to suspend their activities."

"What do you mean? You are talking about Messrs. Delambre and Mechain? The project no longer exists?"

"Oh, it exists. But it's going nowhere. You haven't heard? The Committee of Public Safety has expelled the men on the Committee of Weights and Measures."

"The Committee of Public Safety? What's that? It sounds sinister."

"It is. If you are the wrong sort of people at least."

"Unsafe people?"

"Safe is a very volatile concept these days. Let us say that if you are concerned with your personal safety, it is best not to come to their notice. The commissioners have been found doctrinally unsound. A little lax regarding their republican virtues and hatred of kings. Lacking these vital qualifications for the task at hand, they have been replaced by their students, whose competence is comparable to the scientific validity of your map."

Hence the silence from Paris. Busy stabbing one another in the back, nobody had time to take account of a nonentity stranded in the provinces.

"Then all is lost," I said. "It's over."

Not that it really changed anything for me. I was no longer mapping for the meridian project. I was mapping for my life.

"I doubt it," said Gaspard. "The incompetence of the new appointees is such that even orthodoxy cannot compensate. The real men of science will be brought back in due course. But in the meantime, if I was you, I wouldn't do anything to endanger public safety. Or upset anyone for that matter. If it's not too late for that. Apparently you have already proven adept at upsetting people. In any case, remember. I will be watching you."

Despite not being my most pressing concern, this meddlesome politicking revived and reinvigorated my earlier misgivings, making me wonder whether the meridian project mattered as much as I had believed when I set out. If the best scientific brains in France could be replaced in such an arbitrary fashion by an administration constituted to promote reason, it suggested everything might be arbitrary, that rational aspirations and the quest for precision were chimerical pursuits. This was not mere whimsy on my part, for in making my Murder Map I was indulging in an act of topographical drawing that defied scientific principles, and all the latent doubts that had been lurking inside me were lifting their heads, looking about, and giving voice to their disquiet.

The aim of the expedition for which I had been engaged was to define precisely a uniform, fundamental unit of measurement derived from nature. It was to be the capstone for a process in which scientific precision overcame error, irrational belief, and faulty reasoning. Yet the closer we come to accuracy, the further its attainment recedes, for every refinement reveals the need for ever more minute rectification, so that we are constantly chasing something just beyond our reach. Extreme precision, like extreme passion, is not reasonable. Even extreme reason isn't reasonable. It's simply not human. The same goes for uniformity. It is an ideal that appeals to minds confounded by the pursuit of perfection, minds that cannot countenance the inescapable compromises and ungainly approximations that govern our daily lives. Nature is no help either. Things change, the world is mutable, and when we try to pin it down with uniform or fundamental principles, we lose the quick of it. There is no fundamental value, nothing universal or absolute, only the values we choose to attribute to things.

By contrast with the meridian project, my new map was accessory rather than fundamental, erratic rather than uniform, a work, above all, of impeccable imprecision. It was all made up, which may well be what matters most in life. It's not the punctiliousness with which we gauge the world, but the fantasy we impart to the process of being. I don't wish to be frivolous. That I am frivolous is something I accept unreservedly. It's another lesson I have learned with Marie-Jeanne and her goats. Nevertheless, I was acutely aware that we were dealing with the tragic death of a human being. Yet despite the grievous circumstances and the unscientific nature of the Murder Map, I sensed that it had everything a good map needs. It had a story to tell, an objective to reach, a simplicity of purpose, a vision of the way the world works, no matter how capricious that vision might have been, and it was made to appeal to the imagination, inculcating a sense of wonder, wonder that should shade into fear for the one person above all others at whom it was aimed.

I couldn't have told you all this at the time. Piecing together this memoir, I have realized that writing is thinking. It is only now that I fully comprehend what I dimly apprehended then. But recollecting such intuited presentiments, I have a sneaking affection for the youthful imbecile that I was. And I pity him for the imprudent risks he took as he groped his way toward understanding.

After two more days working up the narrative, I presented the map to Pierre Gaspard.

The next day, the killers declared themselves.

—⁂—

PIERRE GASPARD was confident the meridian project would resume one day and I wanted to make good the delays entailed by my activities in recent weeks, so after clearing it with him I had gone to look for likely triangulation stations farther south in case the arc was extended to Barcelona, a possibility noted in my original brief. Marie-Jeanne had stayed at the farm to grade the recently arrived livestock.

The summit was higher than any I had scaled before and I lingered longer than necessary, admiring the view of the peaks defining the frontier. By the time I started descending, the sun was low in the sky, but there was no cloud cover and the moon was in its first

quarter, so even if night fell, I would have enough light
to make my way back to Tauzet. I was at the foot of
the main rise, beside a muddy spring, when the first
shot was fired.

I heard it quite distinctly, but stupidly failed to
identify it. Even when a murder has been committed,
even when you have made a show of investigating that
murder, you don't expect people to start shooting at
you. I have had the good fortune to avoid serving in
the military, but I would imagine most soldiers find it
equally improbable when they first come under fire.
Me? They're trying to kill ME?!

The second report was followed by a ricochet off a
rock to the right.

Yes, they were trying to kill me. Marie-Jeanne had
been right. If a map made you uneasy, the best way to
deal with the problem was to get rid of the mapmaker.

I bent double and hurried toward a pass above
the spring. I was going south, away from Tauzet, but
the bullets had come from the north as far as I could
tell. Two more shots tore through the fans of broom
shielding my escape, the interval between the two
confirming there was more than one man shooting at
me, unless the killer carried two guns.

The pass gave onto a southern-facing slope covered by a dense sweep of pine where I was able to
stand upright again. I was safe for the present, but
not for long. Once you have tried to shoot a man and
failed, I don't suppose you shrug your shoulders and
say never mind, better luck next time. The logic of
the situation suggests you are committed. And I was
unarmed. All I had was my telescope, the theodolite,
and a pocket knife. I doubted the men who wanted to
kill me would wait about while I whittled them down
to less offensive dimensions.

There were voices behind me. I didn't stop to hear what they were saying. It wasn't the moment for eavesdropping. I pressed on, following a rough trail twisting between the trees. Before long, the ground leveled out, then began to climb, the gradient steepening as the forest deepened and darkened, a close-knit canopy of needles filtering the fading light.

Had I hidden in the woods off path, events might have taken a different turn. It would have been the wisest recourse, waiting till the way was clear then heading back to the village. But I did not like to leave the beaten track, feeling more security in movement than concealment, and so I continued toward the border with Spain.

It was only with the twilight that I took a chance. The tree cover thinned, then the trail climbed toward a crest, crossing an exposed pasture spotted with solitary pine and clumps of gentian. To avoid the open ground, I skirted the southern flank of the pasture, staying close to the tree line. There was no sign of pursuit, but as dark descended I could no longer trust my eyes.

At the top, a perpendicular wall of bare rock defined the western extremity of the pasture. The low moonlight was sufficient to see my way but not so bright as to silhouette me against the pale cliff, encouraging me to venture away from the sheltering woods. At some point, I would have to turn back. But not knowing what was behind me, I continued south, hoping to find a pass into the next valley, or a lateral ridge I could follow until another descent offered itself.

The moon had just set, so it was after midnight when I came to a cluster of shepherds' huts. Shallow structures, no more than waist high, they were made of rough blocks of rock gathered from below the cliffs

and piled in concentric circles, each circle slightly
smaller than the previous one until they met below
a flat coping stone, the cracks roughly caulked with
mud and branches. Scattered firepits still blackened
the ground, but judging by the droppings, wild animals had already reclaimed their demesne, scaveng-
ing any scraps that had been left behind. The thought
made me hungry. I hadn't eaten since morning, fear
and exertion had drained me of energy, and it was
starting to get cold. I could not go much farther, not
fast at least, and exhaustion would make me careless,
so I decided to rest. Even if my pursuers had not yet
given up the chase, they would need to stop as well.
I could hope for a few hours repose.

I placed myself in front of the main hut, my
back against the stones, but as the dew dampened
my clothes and the chill deepened, I realized that a
night in the open air would only weaken me more,
so I crawled into one of the smaller huts, reasoning
that anyone looking for me would inspect the main
dwellings first. The hut must have been used for food
storage. There was a strong smell of cheese and small
mammals scurried for cover when I entered. The old
straw strewn across the floor was greasy, but I was
too tired to care, and curled on the nearside of the
doorway, so that anyone peering through the aperture
would not see me immediately.

I did not sleep. Rather, I was persuaded I did not
sleep, my dreams provoking frequent alarms and the
conviction that I was constantly awake. I only knew
I had slept when I was woken with first light. Not by
first light though. There was a noise outside, footsteps,
and not in my dreams. The footsteps stopped, were
replaced by the sound of shuffling. There was a grunt,

a sigh, the thump of something weighty dropped on
the ground followed by heavy breathing.

—␣◦␣—

THE KILLER was outside. One, at least. There was no
talking, just the heavy breathing. I could remain where
I was, hoping he would go away, but if he didn't,
any advantage would be lost. I eased myself forward.
His pack was in front of the door, bulky enough to
explain the breathing. To the left, the slumped back
of a seated figure: woolen bonnet, broad shoulders,
belted waistband, the curved wooden grip of a pistol
tucked in at the hip.

"Ramond!"

I nearly murdered him with the shock of it. He
jerked upright then scrambled to his feet. Only then
did it occur to me that announcing myself might not
have been a good idea.

"What are you doing here?" he asked.

"Hiding," I said. "Have you come to kill me?"

"Scare me like that again and I will," he said. "But
it's not in my present plans."

"So what are you doing here then?"

"Working. What do you think?" He kicked his pack.
"And you?"

"I told you," I said. "I'm hiding. And running away."

I crawled out of my burrow, of a piece with my
housemates, speckled with fecal matter and strands
of sticky straw. Ramond wrinkled his nose.

"And you thought I was the man trying to kill you,"
he said, once I had explained.

"You weren't very friendly before," I said. "And you
encouraged me to stand in front of Etienne when he
had a gun in his hand."

"There was a time I wouldn't have minded your dying," he admitted. "I saw how my sister looked at you, you know. I'm no fool. It's not easy to think of everything you've known all your life going to another man. The farm, the animals, the land. Everything my family's built up over centuries given to someone else just because I'm younger than Marie-Jeanne. All I've got is what I can make from my back. That and a few friends in the mountains and a . . ."

He stopped abruptly.

"And?"

"I never actively wanted you dead," he said. The shift from what he had to what he had wanted didn't register at the time, but I remembered it later. "And the way you behaved during the duel. I changed my mind. I mean about you and Marie-Jeanne. If anyone can make her happy, it's a lunatic like you."

"Thank you very much."

"Now, though, we better get you out of here. Whoever tried to kill you will be down there waiting. That or they're coming this way now. I'm going into Spain. Your best hope is to come with me. There's a band of *miquelets* up here I do business with. More than business really. Often as not, I live with them. And my . . . Well, if I speak for you, they'll give you a guard, get you back to the village. Marie-Jeanne will be worrying."

The association with the *miquelets* surprised me, for Marie-Jeanne had been most insistent he worked on his own, but I wasn't about to question the legitimacy of anyone who might help me.

"You didn't see her before you left?"

"It was late afternoon," he said, shouldering his pack. "She wasn't expecting you back at that time. Come, the frontier's not far now. We can be there by midday."

Not far, he said. It certainly wasn't far enough for us.

———⁓———

"THAT'S IT," said Ramond. "We've crossed the border."

He eased his pack off his shoulders and I helped lower it to the ground.

The spindly pop of a carbine shot cracked open the silence.

I spun round, looking for the gunmen.

At the second shot, I threw myself down behind the pack.

On the other side of the pack, Ramond was spread-eagled on the ground, a neat hole drilled in the base of his skull. Compared to Etienne's wound, the damage was tidier, but the result was the same. This time, though, the death was my fault, because I was the killers' real target. My gaming with maps had killed my bride's brother.

Two more shots, kicking up dirt on either side of the pack.

I curled into a ball. I had coped with Etienne pointing a pistol at me, but the hole in Ramond's head and the anonymity of his murderers horrified me. Faceless men are far more frightening than a known foe. And I was helpless. I could not revive Ramond, nor avenge him, or even save myself. In the circumstances, the last fact was welcome. How could I face Berenguer, Marie-Jeanne, knowing I was responsible for Ramond's death?

Two more shots, closer.

I pressed myself against the ground.

A bullet buried itself in Ramond's books.

The next went wide, a puff of dust and pebble chips.

I squeezed deeper into the side of the pack.

The pinging sounded too puny to hurt, but a spattering of grit drew blood from my cheek.

Then the shooting stopped, as abruptly as it had begun.

The world went still. A mountain full of prey lay motionless, listening intently.

Had they run out of ammunition?

Remembering Ramond's gun, I peeked past the pack.

A dung beetle labored across the turf between the body and me.

The pistol was on the far side of the body, beyond easy reach.

I heard a muffled command followed by the dull clump of hooves on hard earth.

Each blade of grass was a battleground for the beetle.

The horsemen drew nearer. It was time for me to move.

A miscalculated dandelion leaf tipped the beetle sideways, his little legs waving in the air.

Tack buckles, spur rowels, and curb chains clinked and creaked close by.

The beetle's legs were still waving vainly, like he was bidding me farewell.

It's funny the irrelevant details that become fascinating *in extremis*.

A horse snorted, so near that its breath seemed to warm the back of my neck.

They were too close, it was too late, I had hesitated too long. I rolled over.

I wondered what would happen. To the beetle, I mean. Maybe I should have righted him.

The lead horseman wore a military tailcoat with twin sash belts crossed at the breast of his tunic. Behind him, a squad of *carabineros* had fanned out, riding toward the frontier, scanning the line of the crest. The sergeant reined in his horse.

"*Qué haces?*" he said. "*Qué pasa aquí?*"

The beetle would have to get by on his own.

———∿∿∿———

THE EARLY days of my incarceration passed in a haze of despair. I had never known anything like it, not even during the self-destructive melancholy to which I had succumbed in Paris. I was overwhelmed with remorse and, had the threat of execution, which came later, been proposed at that time, I would have done my utmost to hasten its implementation.

The Spanish soldiers had saved my life. The would-be assassins fled and I was arrested. A corpse detail would be sent to recover the remains of my accomplice, who had clearly been killed by rival smugglers. That's what I was in the soldiers' eyes, a smuggler crouching beside his pack of revolutionary, anticlerical, and pornographic texts. I tried telling them otherwise, that the people pursuing us, the people who had killed Ramond, had been chasing me the mapmaker, not Ramond the smuggler, that they must be the same men who had murdered Etienne, but the soldiers wouldn't listen. The incriminating circumstantial evidence was enough. As far as they were concerned, we were just a bunch of quarrelsome bandits, I was a perfidious and mendacious felon, and the only question to be resolved before proceeding to punishment was whether I also happened to be a spy. Normal smugglers, after all, don't carry telescopes and theodolites. Yet it was this very misapprehension that inadvertently saved my life a second time, for the slow process of determining the precise nature of my crimes meant punishment was postponed.

To begin with, though, I really didn't care what I was accused of or what happened to me as a result. Haunted by the specter of Ramond, I was too busy mortifying myself with regret to worry about my own well-being. The Murder Map had been conceived with the best of intentions, but it had led to the death of one of the very people it was designed to protect. Guilt is a curious thing, being remarkably impervious to logic. Of course, the opposite is true, as well. People will do the most dreadful things and, so long as they believe they behaved badly for virtuous motives, live out their lives with consummate insouciance. But once you have persuaded yourself you have done wrong, no amount of reason will correct the impression. It didn't matter that we had had no other recourse, that I was working to exculpate the Cazalets, that Ramond wasn't meant to be by my side, that he had accompanied me of his own volition in full knowledge of the risks. These were incidentals beside the basic fact that he had been shot by the men trying to kill me.

For the first five months, I was kept on a prison barge at Palamos. My guards were mostly Catalan, so communication was relatively straightforward, but the officers were Castilian and few of them spoke French. As a consequence, my rudimentary Spanish improved greatly, for despite the despondency into which I had fallen, I had to speak when they demanded I repeat for the benefit of successive investigators my story about being a geographical engineer engaged on a peaceful project. Indeed, the interrogation became so familiar and the words came to my tongue so glibly that one

officer accused me of being a Spaniard, thus guilty
of treason too! My Spanish also progressed through
negotiating on behalf of my fellow prisoners.

Principal among those interned on board were two
officers from the merchant marine, Captain Jakob
Krog from Bergen, who had sold his boat and done
something dubious with the proceeds that he preferred not to talk about, and Captain Spiro Calligero from Corfu, whose ship had been impounded
following the discovery of contraband cargo. Captain
Krog was a man of philosophic bent with a pipe permanently clamped between his teeth. He was much
given to lugubrious pronouncements about the hopeless plight of humanity and how we were all doomed,
which made me think it was as well he had sold his
boat. I never did like boats, still less understand them.
All those ropes! And far too unstable, lurching about
with lots of critical bits liable to snap, rupture, and
rip at the most inopportune moments. Above all, they
have a most regrettable habit of sinking in inacces-
sible places. Given their essential implausibility as a
means of transport, you don't want a philosopher in
charge of a ship, especially not a pessimistic one. By
contrast, Captain Calligero was a bubbling cauldron
of excitability (to begin with I thought he was in a
constant rage until I realized it was just his way of
talking) with a tendency to clench his fists and thrust
out his chest when he spoke, as if his heart was about
to burst forth with the tense passion it contained, a
temperament that was probably no better suited to
seafaring than his colleague's morbidity.

There were also three Moroccan ostrich feather
merchants whose only crime was to have been traveling aboard Captain Calligero's boat, a British bible
salesman who could never explain to anyone, least

of all himself, why he was there, and an Ibizan func-
tionary charged with embezzlement who held himself
in such high esteem that he refused to communicate
with anyone else at all, inmates and turnkeys alike.
The rest of our company comprised seven matelots
of uncertain nationality (the incertitude was their
own, possibly their mothers' too), recruited from the
flotsam of Mediterranean ports and imprisoned for
various gradations of piracy, larceny, vagrancy, and
impertinence. Finally, for some unfathomable reason,
our barge also housed half-a-dozen caged monkeys
from Calligero's hold, whose agitated chatter failed to
convince the authorities that they had committed no
crime.

Being better equipped with languages than my
companions, I became a kind of spokesman for the
detainees, and it was this responsibility that, in part,
at least, helped me emerge from my self-indulgent
dejection. Conditions were miserable on board. Bread
was scarce and we were lucky if we got anything to
accompany it beyond a thin gruel of garbanzo beans,
bedding was nothing but straw, and we were all
infested with fleas and lice. Everyone lost weight, most
of all the monkeys, though for pity's sake I insisted
they received appropriate provisions too. The Moroccans said that they had heard of monkeys being eaten
in Africa, causing some of the rougher seamen to
eye the cages speculatively, but despite the poverty
of our diet, I don't think any of us seriously considered sucking the meat off those slender little hands,
the fingers of which were all too human. One man,
who claimed he was a lascar but spoke suspiciously
fluent Italian when he was asleep, conceived such a
liking for the monkeys that, on the memorable occasion when I managed to procure a sack of plantains,

I caught him slipping slices of banana from his own ration through the bars of the cages. As a result of coups like the banana bonanza, I was well liked by the other inmates, and, in making representations to our captors on their behalf, I found that I thought less of myself and the predicament of my own precious conscience, more of practical matters, like ensuring we all survived our ordeal.

This is not to say that I was at ease in myself. I was worried whether Ramond had received a decent burial, for the fort to which the soldiers first took me was some distance from the frontier and I feared wild animals might have desecrated the body before they returned. There were also nagging questions about what was happening across the border. Had Pierre Gaspard made use of my map? Had he caught the people who killed Ramond and Etienne? Were Berenguer and Marie-Jeanne safe, or were they also languishing in jail? These thoughts made me fretful, but they also helped bring me back to life, because I wanted to know the answers.

Then word came that I was to be executed.

—◦◦◦—

LIFE IS partial to pranks like that. It knocks you down, you take dark ages getting back on your feet, then it announces, *Right, that's it, chum, that's your lot, it's all over now.* Why the decision was made, I will never know, but I was informed that I would be transferred to Rosas to await execution for espionage. The reaction of my fellow prisoners was touching. Krog hugged me to his tobacco-cured bosom, gloomily announcing that he had never known a man who less deserved to die, but life was a bitter vale in which the good died young and there was nothing we could do about it, which wasn't particularly heartening of itself, but he meant well. Calligero started wailing, the Moroccans clasped my hands and offered to commend me to Mohammed, promising all manner of improbable pleasures in the life to come, the matelots began beating their chests so hard that I had to beg them to desist before they did themselves some permanent damage, the bible salesman was so overcome that he declared it a "dashed shame" (I never did understand what he meant by that), the monkeys set up a cacophony so ear-piercingly shrill that I almost wished we had eaten them after all, and even the Ibizan was moved to give me a commiserating pat on the shoulder, although he wiped his hand on the straw afterward. But lamentation is not the language of bureaucracy and I was duly removed to Rosas.

My second jail was less crowded and more salubrious than the first. I was lodged on my own in a small, windowless chapel on the hills behind the port, and provided with a rope bed, a rickety table, and a rush chair. Why I was placed there, I do not know, but it was a peculiar prison for someone hitherto accused of smuggling blasphemous books. When I asked Don Manuel de Vacaro about it, he just opened his arms and turned his eyes skyward, like an exasperated Madonna, as if to say this was one of the more widespread and least explicable of life's many mysteries . . . a slightly odd response since he was the commander in charge of my confinement.

Don Manuel was a strange man, very prim and proper, thin to the point of emaciation, the only fat thing about him being a magnificently tailored mustache that must have taken hours of meticulous topiary every morning, but he was always fidgeting, giving the impression that his uniform was too small so that it chafed his private parts. I don't think he was really cut out for a military career. When he heard I claimed to be a man of science, he came to visit me, for he, too, was "a fellow savant," as he put it. I did not disabuse him about my credentials on the sagacity front. Unwarranted esteem was the least of my worries.

Don Manuel had a pet theory. Most savants do. He believed water was a foolproof panacea for all maladies, so that one only had to get the dosage right to sluice out every disease and debility to which humankind was subject. He said this with a jar of wine at his side, a beverage he never failed to bring with him on his visits, and which he urged me to drink while he talked. Maybe he was trying to kill me before the hangman got to me. I listened politely anyway. Indeed, I had nothing else to do, apart from wait for death. And there was a certain charm to the fractured French he insisted on using, being "a man of science" himself.

Don Manuel's theory was posited on the idea that, since water is the principal component of our vital organs, our muscles, and above all our blood, it stood to reason that any physical infirmity was consequent on the lack of this indispensable element. He had proof. He had studied it himself. Heartburn, lumbago, arthritis, asthma, rheumatism, migraine, piles, epilepsy, colic, diabetes, obesity, consumption, constipation. Through the judicious administration of water, he had resolved the underlying corporeal drought that was responsible for all these conditions.

"Here, have some wine," he said. "Do you suffer any particular point of ill health yourself, Señor Darbon?" He seemed quite hopeful, but apart from the obvious, imminent fatality, I was unable to oblige. "A pity," he said. "I might have cured you. But perhaps in the circumstances."

I wondered whether "the circumstances" had anything to do with the startling success of his method, whether his experiments had always involved condemned men, who were, in the nature of these things, infallibly cured of all earthly ailments.

"That's all it needs?" I asked, taking a sip of my wine. "Water?"

"And salt," he said. "Some conditions require salt too."

He topped up my glass.

"Shouldn't I be drinking water?"

"You are to be hanged, Señor Darbon. It is not important anymore. But if you had been sick, I would have remedied the problem. Indubitably. One must never die in poor health."

Sometimes I had my doubts about Don Manuel's sanity, all that water notwithstanding.

"And that's all then? Water and salt?"

"And no food. You must drink the water on an empty stomach. Here, have wine."

I had the empty stomach at least. Don Manuel had supplied me with a large clay pot of rice secured by a very nice lid. Unfortunately, in his enthusiasm for water and no solids, he had neglected to provide any means of cooking the stuff. I did mention this to him, but he waved my caviling aside, as if this were a minor detail not worthy of consideration by men of science. In the early days, I only survived thanks to the kindness of my guards, who readily shared their own meals with me.

For all his eccentricities, I enjoyed my talks with Don Manuel. He seemed to enjoy them, too, possibly because nobody else would listen to him. He visited nearly every day, sometimes bringing a chess set with him, a game for which I had no aptitude, but he didn't mind beating me with monotonous regularity, and a peculiar friendship developed between us, one premised on passing the time as much as anything more profound. I don't suppose many condemned men have enjoyed such a privileged relationship with their principal jailer.

I got on well with my guards too. They were not soldiers, but peasants from the village of Cadaqués. They let me sit outside with them and I would question them about their lives, their homes, their community. Guilelessly, they told me everything, all the scandals, the relationships, the rivalries, the different roles played by different families, who was a scold, who was lazy, who drank too much, who neglected ancient dependents. When a new batch of guards arrived from the same village, I amused myself by telling them I was a traveling merchant who had once visited Cadaqués and recounted all I had heard from the other guards. They were so impressed by the details that they decided I had not merely visited but was really a former resident in disguise, the son of the apothecary, who had gone to America years ago to make his fortune, been caught returning by an illicit route, and that I was now lying about my identity to hide my money. I protested, but they were having none of it, and took my denials for further proof of my sly acumen. All in all, I was earning a wholly unmerited reputation for sapience in Spain.

The next day my "aunt" came to see me, instantly claiming to recognize me, and reminding me how she used to dandle me on her knee when I was a small boy. I didn't like to disappoint her. It would not have been kind. She said my "merchant" ruse was good, that I should keep it up until I was released, which I surely would be, and in the meantime she would provide me with food. In the coming weeks, each new guard detail arrived with a hamper full of cold chicken, cured sausage, boiled eggs, salt fish, fresh cheese, dark olives, and dry fruit. I now shared my meals with the guards rather than the other way round and had such a surfeit that I was obliged to ask them to take food home to their families, thus effecting a satisfying redistribution of wealth in the village. Don Manuel did not seem unduly troubled or indeed puzzled by my inexplicably well-stocked larder, despite its unhealthful properties. Such miraculous bounty was doubtless the due of men belonging to the fraternity of science and one didn't question its provenance.

The Spanish are a very endearing people and I still think of them with affection. But they were an endearing people intent on killing me, or at the very least duty bound to do so, and in due course the day of my execution arrived.

I WAS woken in the middle of the night. Don Manuel was at the door looking very solemn in full regalia. He was wearing a feathered tricorne hat and had a ceremonial sword hanging from a tasseled baldric. He had taken particular care with his mustache. The tips could take your eye out if he had been of a mind to kiss you and the central parting was so perfect that I suspect he had been plucking stray hairs. In one hand he held a small hessian sack, in the other an oil lamp.

"It is very sad," he said.

"It is?" I said.

"It is," he said, then paused, apparently at a loss for words.

"It is very late," I said.

"It is never too late," he said.

There was another long pause.

"Would you like some water?" I asked.

The threat of water was enough to prompt him to speech.

"I regret to inform you," he said, "that today is the day you must die. It is official. The governor, he has proclaimed it. You are dead."

I didn't know what to say. Neither, it seemed, did Don Manuel.

"It is very sad," he repeated.

There was a silence I felt constrained to fill if only to help him out of his predicament.

"Well, it comes to us all, I suppose," I said.

The door was open. There were no guards outside, no soldiers.

"Yes," said Don Manuel, mournfully. "Things come to us all. I have always said this."

He nodded at the doorway in a distracted way, looked at me meaningfully.

"Is there anything I can do for you?" I asked. He really did seem at a loss.

He stared at me a little longer. A slight tremor twitched the tips of his mustache.

"I am very sorry to report . . . you have escaped."

"I have?"

"Very, very sad."

He jerked his head at the open door again, then stared into a corner of the room. He was quite downcast by the news of my flight.

"Escaped, you say?"

"Yes. You are not here. You have gone. Disappeared. Vanished. Evaporated. Like water on a hot plate. Indubitably. The guard, he did not lock the door. He brings your meal and he leaves open the door. He is very negligent. He will be punished."

"Not too harshly, I hope."

"It will be very harsh," he said, still scrutinizing the corner forlornly. "Very, very harsh."

He glanced at me briefly, winked once, then returned his gaze to the wall. The mustache quivered, struggling with an emotion all of its own.

"He will drink water," he said. "For his improvement. For a full month."

"He will drink water?" I said.

"Yes, water. Lots of it. We must cure his negligence. We men of science have our tribulations to bear, our duties to fulfill. I am sure you will understand. It is not important how far apart we are. The international brotherhood of scholarship binds us together."

It was a hard road to travel.

Don Manuel held out the sack, a parting gift. I took it and I walked out while he stared into the distance, his only farewell a deep sigh at the abominable injustices of the world and the many trials suffered by men of science, not least the mysteries of miraculously disappearing prisoners.

—⁓—

I sometimes wonder how Spain ever muddled its way into an empire. I don't suppose the Aztecs would have had such a rough time had Don Manuel been the main man in the tin hat, and I can't imagine the simple folk of Cadaqués rampaging their way across the continent. Yet that is one of life's real mysteries, how the kindest of peoples can transform themselves into killing machines when governed by greed, stupidity, pride, or fear. It is something even a connoisseur of absurdity has difficulty comprehending. All I can say is that my experience of Spaniards was very different.

I was not, however, so naive as to suppose everyone would welcome a passing stranger. I concealed myself during the day, hiding in abandoned barns, remote woods, and the uninhabited hinterland, only traveling at night, following obscure trails traversing the hills behind the coast, the silvery sea sprawling below me like a marbled looking glass. The sack Don Manuel had given me contained food, readily edible food like almonds, figs, and ham (his convictions were not so dogmatic after all), but I was careful not to eat too much of it, preferring instead to pilfer what I could from unguarded gardens, root cellars, smokehouses, and orchards, since constraints on open travel meant I had at least two weeks walking ahead of me, and needed to conserve my provisions.

I had been away for more than eight months and I had done a lot of thinking in that time, or at least what passed for thinking with me in those days. It was these thoughts, even more than my responsibilities as the prisoners' representative or the kindness of my captors in Rosas, that eventually revived my spirits. I could not bring Ramond back. That tragedy would stand and I would have to live with it for the rest of my days. But I could strive to make good the want, not by supplanting him, but by supplementing the lives of the people he had left behind. Above all, I would make my life something it had never promised to be in the past.

My previous fantasies had always involved proving myself on a large scale, achieving fame, fortune,
freedom through intellectual endeavor and academic
daring. I had nearly frittered away that hope with my
feckless behavior in Paris. The meridian project had
given me a second chance. But when you take the
measure of the world you generally end up evaluating
things you didn't intend computing in the first place
and coming to conclusions quite contrary to expecta-
tion. In the experiences of the preceding year, I had
realized that fame and fortune are fickle and incidental, that freedom is relative, and that even the adventure of scientific discovery is nothing if not rooted in
something more elementary—not in the sense of first
principals or primary matter, nothing is more elementary than science in those terms, but in the concept
of what I can only call groundwork.

The adventurer skates over life, he is never fixed,
always in movement, fleeing what he perceives to be
limits in pursuit of freedom. But freedom does not
reside in individual prowess or personal liberty. To
have meaning, it must be collective. It must come from
the alignment of singular sensibilities finding common
ground in a shared reality. And this demands limits.
Limits are not the same as confinement. I know, I
have been confined, both by myself inside my mind,
and by others in my body. I was lucky, neither confinement crippled me, but I have experienced confinement enough to know the difference. True limits are
simply what we are given, they are the code within
which we operate, the meter of the verse we live. I
am not talking about the limits imposed on us from
above, those societal and political restrictions that
my generation aimed to dismantle, but the limits of
time, space, intellect, and emotion, the whole poetic

structure of our lives, the form and integrity of which are damaged when we believe we can live beyond the brink. Perhaps the greatest risk of a life without limits is transience, the notion that we can use up one place, then move on, use up other people, then move on, use up the world about us, then move on, because when we feel we can escape to somewhere else, we will neglect and spoil what we have instead of nurturing it with a proper respect.

To counter this and to make something of myself and my relations with the people I loved, I had to fix myself in place and concentrate on the reality of the life around me; I had to become a husbandman of the land and learn to listen to the music of the immediate world. It never quite happened like that, of course. Things never do. But what did happen was close enough, which is also the usual way of things.

First, though, I had to go home.

———

UNTIL THE end, the alarms of my journey were modest and need not be enumerated. The only moment when I was seriously concerned came in the Upper Ampurdan. It was in the early hours of the morning and I was trudging along a mountain track when two men emerged from the trees, each carrying a carbine. That is as much as I know of them. I didn't linger long enough to take in any details of dress or physiognomy. Men with guns were men to avoid, especially in the middle of the night. If they were soldiers or militiamen, I wanted nothing to do with them; and if they were brigands, I didn't trust to poverty to protect me from their disappointment when they found my pockets were empty. I plunged into the woods and

started tearing through the trees, descending a pre-
cipitous slope.

Whatever their initial intentions, this declaration
of distrust was enough to aggravate their animosity.
There were shouts and curses, a shot was fired. I kept
running, cutting across to the right to distance myself
from my original trajectory. I had thought that would
be enough, that they would not persist in their pursuit of a solitary traveler on foot, but they were determined, or more desperate than me. I could hear them
ranging back and forth through the woods, calling to
one another. The chances of their cornering me in the
night were slim, but my fright was such that reason
took flight faster than I did, so that when I saw a light
lower down in the valley, I resolved to seek sanctuary
with whoever was there.

Reaching the farm, I rapped on the door. There
was silence, no voices, not even a dog barking, but the
lamp still burned brightly. I knocked again. "Open up,
in the name of the king," I cried. This was risky. The
last time I'd acted in the name of a king was in Vauriennes and his patronage hadn't done me any good
at all. But as Pascal wisely observed, latitude changes
everything, and what is right on one side of the Pyrenees is wrong on the other. The door opened.

Inside there were three startled-looking women
ranging through the generations: one withered and
wizened, one plump and in her prime, the third pushing past pubescence into maturity. The absence of men
comforted me, not because of any predatory instinct
or because I believed I was the stronger party (mas-
culine strength is one of the great myths of history;
I never did understand why fortitude is measured by
muscle power alone), but because I believed women
would be more likely to offer refuge to a fugitive.

Looking back on it, I'm not sure why I thought this, for I have since seen women behave every bit as callously as men, but on that occasion my instinct was sound. The moment I explained I was being pursued by footpads, my guardian angels barred the door and doused the lamp. I wanted to weep. It was not just the immediate succor, but the isolation of the preceding days, the haunting sense of being proscribed, perhaps even hunted, had weighed heavy on my nerves.

We had an uncomfortable night, silently sitting in the dark, waiting, listening, watching the shadows, the only relief a dim glow from the fading embers in the grate. The windows were not glazed and several times we heard something large blundering through the woods, whether a wild boar or my pursuers, we did not know, but there was one moment when there were distinct albeit distant voices. Nobody came to the house though.

Before I left the next day, I asked why a light had been burning so late. It transpired that the pig had been slaughtered that morning and the women had been preparing the black pudding. It was very good black pudding too. They gave me a length to take with me. It is a chastening thought that I may owe my life to the death of a pig. Even more striking is the idea that I might have died but for the boiling of a blood sausage. I like to reflect on that when I suspect I am becoming too self-important. Everybody ought to have their own blood sausage to bring them down to earth and balance out their vanity. And, of course, to remind them that the most mundane items can have incalculable importance. There are many ways in which a blood sausage may be your savior.

Once in the Albères, the more elaborate precautions of my voyage so far were no longer necessary, as

I was close by the French frontier, so I could chance traveling by daylight. I might have descended into my homeland directly, but I had no documents, having left my *laissez passer* in Tauzet, which had in any case been in the king's name, so I reckoned it safer to stick to the untenanted uplands. I was right, too, for though I did not know it at the time, a few months earlier a decree had been issued requiring French citizens to have a passport to travel in the interior of the country. Unfortunately, some authorities are not fastidious about documentation, considering questions of liberty and custody matters for their own discretion, regardless of legal niceties.

Six days had passed since I turned inland from the Mediterranean. I had successfully negotiated the delicate crossing of the *Grande Route* between Perpignan and Barcelona, avoided detection by the garrison in the Bellegarde fortress, and passed to the south of the Massif du Canigou via a mine trail. I was entering the Pyrenees proper and preparing myself for the descent to my destination. I was nearly there, Tauzet was no longer a distant dream, but an imminent reality, a little over a day's walk away, and in my excitement to find the answers to all my questions, I grew careless. I was tramping across a grassy pass, my mind lost in a trance of anticipation, enjoying the hollow thump of my feet on the turf when a man with a gun appeared in front of me.

This was too much! I actually felt quite cross. Didn't these people have homes to go to?

A dozen more figures emerged from the rocks on either side of me.

On this occasion, there was no pugnacious mule to come to my defense, nowhere to run, no sheltering darkness or haven of trees, no convenient sorority offering sanctuary.

I raised my hands, wondering where I would find my blood sausage this time.

I don't mean to be disrespectful, but the blood sausage came in the shape of a small girl.

—∿—

ONCE THE bandits, who were Catalan Spaniards, had confirmed I was as penniless as I claimed, there was a brief confabulation about my fate. The talk was not reassuring. One or two were ready to let me go, but others argued it was too risky. They didn't want their whereabouts revealed to the authorities. It would be as well to kill me and have done with it. Moderating voices suggested taking me back to their camp, for my claim to be a government surveyor made them think I might fetch a ransom. The poor sap-heads. Even the most august savant is meanly valued by bureau-crats and the idea that any administration, still less one convulsed by revolution, would pay more than a couple of *sous* for someone like me smacked of ter-minal mental derangement. I didn't say so though. In the short term, doubtless very short, the hope of a ransom was the best I could do by way of a blood sausage.

The argument went back and forth, but nobody was in a hurry to do the actual killing, nor to take responsibility for my release, so the ransom men won the day. Blindfolded, my wrists bound and knotted to a tether, I was led away from the pass. After about an hour of fitful, stumbling progress, the blindfold was removed. The sudden light made me shield my eyes until the dazzle faded. The first thing I saw when my vision cleared was the girl.

She was small, maybe five years old, but scrawny for any age. Her skin was tawny, the natural darkness deepened by woodsmoke, sun, and wind. She was pretty, but there was something pinched, almost covert in her regard, a wariness verging on withdrawal. It was the face of someone wounded beyond her years. That did not explain my response though. The instant I saw her, I felt profoundly uneasy. She was familiar, but a stranger at the same time. Above all, I had the impression that looking at her was in some manner indecent. I turned aside.

The bandits' camp was well placed. It was at the top of a steep pasture, the grass so coarse that I doubted it was ever used by domestic flocks, even at the height of summer. Above the pasture, a cliff rose to a sharp pinnacle. Between the pasture and the pinnacle, a long lip of rock shielded a broad depression, behind which there was the mouth of a cave, invisible from below. The cave was the keep of their stronghold while the lip of rock formed a curtain wall that curved up to narrow gateways at either end of the cliff, so the gang could not be cornered inside what was in effect the bailey. The site was concealed, easily defended, and easily escaped.

It was late afternoon when we arrived. I was taken into the cave, hands still bound, and lodged in a natural chamber at the back of the redoubt. There seemed to be dozens of these secondary dens, some larger than others, several lit by pitch brands. Mine had no light except what seeped in from the torches outside. My tether was tied to a rock. I was given a beaker of water and a bowl of cold porridge. I might have freed myself, the rope was only loosely attached to the rock, but the main cavern was filling up as evening advanced. I doubted I could escape and any thwarted attempt would inevitably have negative consequences.

I slept poorly that night, not merely because of my predicament and the frustration of being detained so close to my objective, but because I couldn't get the girl out of my mind. She was only a child, yet the look of her had been intensely unsettling. It was as if she reminded me of someone, but the familiarity felt improper, like seeing the shadow of your mother in a lover. I did not, of course, feel any lust for her. I had heard of men who had such tastes. There were houses in Paris that catered to their wretched appetites. The very idea repelled me. But the girl's face had triggered a memory that was in some measure tainted by an inappropriate passion.

The next morning, I was taken out to discover my fate. My fate and that of the child, too.

—◦◦◦—

THE MEN who had apprehended me were absent, but five others were sitting in a semicircle on an arc of conveniently located boulders, and in the distance, just beyond the bailey, several women were slapping wet clothing against a sheet of rock beside a torrent.

"What's happening," I said to the man leading me. It looked suspiciously like a tribunal.

"Barbu wants to speak to you," said my jailer.

There was no mistaking Barbu. The man at the center of the tribunal was blessed with the most enormous black beard, so deep and thick that you might almost have imagined he had skinned a bear and hooked the hide over his ears. It was logical, of course, that he should be named after his principal attribute. He wouldn't want outsiders knowing his real name.

"You are bandits, aren't you?" I said, puzzled by my impression that these men were presiding over a mock legal procedure.

My guard turned quickly, knitting his brows and pursing his lips, as if I had made a rude noise. He drew himself up a little, braced his shoulders.

"We," he said, with ceremonial emphasis, "are *miquelets*."

I wouldn't make that mistake again. It might prove fatal.

I had understood that *miquelets* were militiamen who conducted the odd robbery on the side rather than professional brigands. Consequently, had you told me I was about to meet some, I would have expected, if not a uniform, at least some form of insignia. But scanning the present assembly, a more ragtag rabble would be hard to imagine. Barbu managed to be a motley all in himself. He wore filthy white military breeches, but his calves were bare. Each foot was clad in what looked like the best part of a lamb, so roughly cobbled together that you could be forgiven for thinking he had raided the sheepfold, selected a couple of creatures that looked about the right size, and just pulled them on. He wore a thick linen shirt, a sheepskin jerkin, a bright blue Phrygian bonnet, and, just visible on either side of his beard, a voluminous red neckerchief long since bleached pink by the elements. The color scheme made him look like a tatty flag. On legs. I kept this to myself.

"So, Señor Geographical Engineer," he said, "speak up for yourself. Any particular reason we should not kill you?"

This was not an auspicious start. Barbu's voice was as deep and ursine as his beard, and the contempt he injected into the epithet made me cringe inside. There was nothing for it though. I repeated my story, how I was a man of no importance (I no longer placed any confidence in the ransom fantasy) who had had the misfortune to be taken prisoner by the Spanish army due to a regrettable case of mistaken identity, since happily resolved, that I was somebody who had nothing against *miquelets* (a word I pronounced as if it were an honorable title much prized by the most reputable men), indeed rather admired them for I had heard many good things about their integrity and magnanimity, and if it so pleased him, I would now like to continue on my way to reach my loved ones, among whom there was nobody who resembled anything like an official responsible for enforcing the iniquitous laws of foreign lands.

Barbu was not impressed by my performance, understandably so. In my anxiety to ingratiate myself, I had been virtually groveling, and the stuff about how wonderful the *miquelets* were was such transparent flattery it almost flipped into insult. He conferred briefly with his companions, a bit too briefly for my tastes, then looked at me again.

"I believe we will kill you," he said. He spoke softly, but words like that don't need accentuating to have an impact. At least I did not quail. I had been here before. "But not here and not today," he continued. "We don't want to bother ourselves digging a hole for you."

He was right. I could do that all on my own.

At that moment, the girl happened to pass behind the tribunal. Despite her age, she was at work, carrying a pail of dirty bowls toward the torrent where the women were washing clothes. She was so frail that she could barely stay upright with the weight, even though the bowls were only wood.

"Who is that child?" I asked without thinking.

Barbu and his men looked at me a little surprised.

"Nuria?" he said. "What matter is it to you?"

None, really. But if I was to die, I'd like to know why she troubled me so.

"You shouldn't make her work like that," I said. "She's too young."

This was a step too far. Barbu jumped to his feet, the bear-like qualities spreading from his beard to his brow. Maybe he would take the trouble to dig that hole after all. And then it hit me: the child! That face, those eyes, the quality of the expression hiding behind the hurt, the carriage even at such a young age. And I remembered the last conversation I had had in France before I was taken prisoner by the Spaniards. I looked Barbu in the eyes.

"Do you, by any chance, know someone called Ramond Cazalet?"

—⁓—

NURIA SAVED my life that day. She was "too young." Too young for me to identify her resemblance to her aunt, but not too young for that resemblance to stir uneasy feelings in me. My wild surmise had been correct. These were the *miquelets* with whom Ramond had lived.

Once I had explained my relationship to that unhappy man, my captors' attitude toward me changed comprehensively. A little too comprehensively for comfort. Barbu opened his arms wide and drew me to his chest in what I can only describe as a bear hug. He held me tight and squeezed. I could hear vertebrae cracking and the hiss of expelled air. For a moment, I thought he might need to proceed with his plans for the hole, because I was suffocating in his beard, and if the beard didn't do the job, the overpowering stench of stale sweat and old smoke would probably finish me off regardless. When he eventually released me, I was gasping, and only a large dose of brandy jolted me back into wheezy breathing.

Several of the *miquelets* had helpmeets in the mountains with them and Ramond had followed their example. Only he had gone one better. He had won the heart of Barbu's sister. The relationship was passionate, but short lived. Montse died giving birth to Nuria. Hearing this, I remembered what Berenguer had said about Ramond, the guilt he had harbored concerning his own mother's death, how his anger at the world had worsened since he took up smuggling. He had killed his mother and killed his lover by the same method. No wonder he was surly. I also recalled Marie-Jeanne insisting he wasn't a *miquelet*, as if that were an insult, which would explain why he had kept his liaison secret from the family.

Barbu had a rough affection for his niece, but even the most insensate individual could see that living in a cave with a gang of vagabonds whose vocation was war and malfeasance was no life for a small child. I put it more politely than that though. Then I told him about Berenguer and Marie-Jeanne, about their kindliness and the warmth of the welcome they had offered me, about the relative wealth, comfort, and security of their home. I told him all this hoping it was still true, but there was no point muddying the issue with pessimistic speculation. I had to try. If nothing else, I owed it to Ramond to ensure his daughter had the best chance in life possible, and I hoped that bringing her back to the family would in some measure compensate for his death.

Barbu agreed. Beard or no, I kissed him when he gave his assent. You may not know this, but bears can blush too. For a nasty moment, I thought he might embrace me again, but he mastered himself sufficiently to reach for the brandy bottle instead.

I stayed with my newfound friends for another week, nurturing an incipient complicity with Nuria. We were together all the time. During the day, we roamed the mountains, just as I had with Marie-Jeanne. I asked her to show me her favorite places and we made a small map of them on a scrap of parchment, scratching out the locations with fragments of charcoal from the fire. We played games, skipping stones across the lake that nestled behind the pinnacle, building boulder men and knocking them down, making daisy chains to decorate one another, racing deliciously errant dung beetles, stalking marmot, not to kill them but to see how close we could get, laughing helplessly when the creatures fled, tumbling over one another and tripping on protruding rocks. We staged races between ourselves, too, races I always contrived to lose, complaining loudly how outrageously unfair it was, that she must be cheating in some obscure way. She knew it wasn't true, knew too that that was the point of it, what made my protests droll. We had tremendous fun flinging dry cow pats at each other, then found a water chute in the torrent where we could slither down into a plunge pool before scrambling back to the top giggling like . . . well, like children.

That's one of the great things about children. Where they play, adults occasionally play too. I pity people who do not have the opportunity for child's play. It's not that we learn from it, but we recover what we have forgotten. Nuria was the first of many children who would bring me back to that value of attentiveness I have spoken of elsewhere. Her concentration on every game was complete. She was there in that moment, not looking ahead or glancing over her shoulder, her whole being crammed into an instant of eternity.

I also told her stories, stories about my life in the orphanage, a motherless child like her, stories about Molly, the Bottom Biting Mule (she liked them), stories about the great things her father had done, which made her sad and proud at the same time, stories about all the adventures she might have in her future life. I told her about her aunt and grandfather, how kind they were and how pleased they would be to meet her, about the freedoms and comforts she would enjoy in her new home, and about the secret places I would in turn show her near Tauzet. At night I taught her the stars and showed her how she could locate herself in the world by looking at the heavens. I was doing much the same for myself.

It wasn't all straightforward. It took time to overcome her suspicions, to find a way through the maze of fear and loss that had been the reality of her life hitherto, and when we finally left, she wept (I won't even begin to tell you how sodden Barbu's beard was), crying for everything and everyone she was leaving behind, for despite the hardships, it was all she had known, and there had been moments of tenderness to alleviate the privation. But she did not ask to stay. She had learned enough hope to carry her away from her old home and family. Only there was no knowing if that hope was justified. It would be a cruel trick to promise another life if that life no longer existed. I had had to keep it simple though. *Maybe* is no way to inspire a child. Children need certainty, no matter how illusory. *Maybes* are for the adults to deal with.

The same questions remained.

Had the Murder Map done anything but get Ramond killed?

Had the killers been caught?

Were Berenguer and Marie-Jeanne at liberty?

Was the life I had promised still possible?

—⁓—

I HAD to clutch Nuria's shoulder for support. Berenguer was standing in front of the barn, rubbing Molly down with a worn brush. The mule brayed a greeting. Berenguer turned to face us. He had aged ten years in as many months. Still holding onto Nuria, I urged her forward. She was shy, abashed by the presence of this fabled man. Berenguer's eyes flitted between the two of us then settled on Nuria, watching her intently. Off to the right, there was a grassy mound with a cross planted at its head. Berenguer glanced back at me, saw where I was staring.

"Ramond," he said. "His body was found . . ."

"I know," I said, glad neither the soldiers nor the wild animals had got to him first. "I was with him. The men who killed Etienne. They were hunting me. Ramond was helping me escape. They shot him."

Berenguer bit his lower lip, looked down at the ground, back up at me.

"They were caught," he said. "Your map. The magistrate said it showed who killed Vidal. Two foresters fled. Ferran and Theo. The militia overtook them near the border. They confessed."

I remembered the names. They were two of the men Etienne had obliged to participate in my triangulation display. There was a moment's silence, then Berenguer turned his attention back to Nuria.

"And who is this young lady?" he asked.

Despite the quickened aging, his smile was as kindly and courteous as ever.

"Nuria," I said. "Your granddaughter."

Berenguer's body jolted upright, as if a muscular spasm had plumbed his spine. He was confused. Understandably. He half turned toward the house, then back to Nuria. She raised her eyes, smiled timidly.

"I'll let her explain," I said.

Recovering his composure, Berenguer held out his hand.

"Do you like animals, Nuria?"

She nodded. He smiled again.

"Perhaps we could brush Molly here a bit and have ourselves a talk."

Nuria's mouth opened and her eyes snapped to Molly. The discovery that this was the celebrated Bottom Biting Mule made all the difference.

"Marie-Jeanne?" I said.

"She's indoors," said Berenguer, taking Nuria by the hand, "but . . ."

"No, let me surprise her."

He placed the brush in Nuria's hand, cupping her tiny fist in his palm to demonstrate the correct direction for currying Molly's coat.

"There's a surprise for you too," he said, carefully.

"Later," I said.

I gave Nuria an encouraging smile, but she was lost to me. She was busy. She was brushing Molly with a solemn absorption that might have been comical had it not been so touching.

"So where have you been living, Nuria?" asked Berenguer.

The inside of the farm was dark, but the kitchen shutters were open, channeling a shaft of mote-filled light onto the chair where Marie-Jeanne was sitting. She caught her breath when she saw me, her lips shaping a perfect O. She stared at me for a moment, then let her gaze drop to her lap. My turn to gape, gulping like a beached fish. Marie-Jeanne was cradling a baby. The baby had the most beautiful green eyes.

"A boy or a girl?" I said, when I could trust my voice not to quaver.

"A girl."

Those eyes!

"She's lovely," I said. "Her sister is outside."

"Her sister?"

"Well, strictly speaking her cousin. But when we marry."

"We will marry?"

Marie-Jeanne seemed amused.

"We will," I said.

"There'll be a *charivari,*" she said. "You know that?"

"There's a price to pay for most things."

"No ordinary one, not with this one here."

She nodded at Etienne's daughter, our daughter.

"That's no problem," I said, reaching for the baby. "I can do donkeys."

Fibbing and Pilfering

The Measure of the World is a fiction and assumes fiction's rights to play fast and loose with what passes for factual truth. Among the creative untruths I have allowed myself are the following:

My story takes place between the summers of 1791, when the National Assembly approved the principle of a meridian-based measure, and 1792, when the historical meridian expedition began. The expedition did not use scouts like the narrator (and would never have employed someone who had flunked his studies), though similar work was done by Jean Joseph Tranchot (1752–1815), a cartographic engineer and much put-upon assistant to the astronomer in charge of the southern stretch of the meridian, Pierre Mechain (1744–1804).

Marianne, the emblem of the Republic, did not make an appearance until 1792, though characters with the same name and similar attributes existed in popular and literary culture before then. As far as I am aware, Louis XVI was not dubbed "Citizen Capet" until his trial at the end of 1792. Likewise, revolutionary paranoia about spies and external enemies only really developed in the same year, when war with Austria and Prussia broke out.

I have exaggerated the lack of mapping in Languedoc-Roussillon. The region had been mapped by the Cassini dynasty, while the Pyrenees were mapped by the king's engineer Roussel (d.1733) and François de la Blottière (1673–1739), who did a better job than I suggest in the text. The Pyrenees were no longer as isolated as I make out, recent road-building having opened up the region, tying it more closely to France. Consequently, many of the customary rights and traditional loyalties in the mountains were already disappearing before the revolution put an end to them.

The allusion to the ritual observation of royalty refers to Louis IV. His successors avoided the oppressive and intrusive ceremonies that circumscribed the private lives of earlier monarchs. The suspension of the meridian project's leaders on doctrinal grounds actually happened three years later. The Committee of Public Safety was not established until 1793. Relations with Spain were not hostile when my story unfolds. There were concerns about the influx of "French" ideas, notably in the form of smuggled texts as described in the novel, but scientific neutrality was respected even in times of war. Scholarly cooperation declined when Napoleon embarked on his European tour, but in 1792 it is unlikely that a man of science would have languished so long in jail.

I have used many Anglo-Saxon terms rather than adhering to a strictly Latinate vocabulary and syntax.

As a rule, I have avoided words and coinages that postdate the period, but French speakers will notice one or two instances where a word has been analyzed etymologically despite the fact that it wouldn't have been used in this sense in French. For example, though "survey" comes from French, the topographic meaning is purely English.

That's it as far as conscious falsehoods go, though doubtless specialists will be cringing at undetected errors. That's the price of knowing too much. In the meantime, I must make my acknowledgments.

The narrator's story was inspired by several historical figures, above all the life of Jacques-François Loiseleur Deslongchamps (1747–1843) (m. Marie-Jeanne Boudou in 1774) and the misadventures of François Arago (1786–1853), the latter detailed in his *Histoire de Ma Jeunesse*. I have also appropriated certain mishaps that befell Mechain and Jean-Baptiste Delambre (1749–1822), the astronomer charged with the northern stretch of the meridian. Details of Deslongchamps's life can be found (in French) on the Internet at the following address:

> https://aveyron.com/histoire-culture/fameux-rouergats/
> jacques-francois-loiseleur-deslongchamps.

Having only ever passed two sets of maths and science exams in my life, the ones to get into secondary school and the ones to get out of it (my motivation was strong), tackling this subject matter was presumptuous in the extreme. I did a lot of reading and still only had a hazy idea of the complicated calculations involved in mapping and measuring the world.

For more informed reading on the subject, see Ken Alder's *The Measure of All Things,* a marvel of erudition and immaculately orchestrated narrative detailing Delambre and Mechain's work on the meridian arc. Edward Danson's *Weighing the World* is a superior piece of popular scholarship by a professional surveyor describing developments during the enlightenment, particularly in the English-speaking world. Simon Garfield's *On the Map* is a breezy overview of cartography throughout history. Josef Konvitz's *Cartography in France 1660–1848* is a well-researched monograph that does what it says on the label. Michèle Porte's essay, *La naissance du mètre—L'invention du vide,* is a fascinating summary of a seminar that owes as much to its author's psychoanalytical and anthropological learning as her mathematical training. Graham Robb's wide-ranging, well-written, and consistently stimulating *The Discovery of France* first alerted me to the story of Deslongchamps. Anthropological details about life in the Pyrenees were culled from *La Vie Quotidienne dans les Pyrenees sous l'Ancien Regime* by Jean-François Soulet, part of a wonderful series now largely out of print but available through secondhand-book dealers on the Internet. I don't doubt that it is outdated, and I wouldn't be surprised if contemporary historians howl with horror at the idea of relying on it as a principal source, but as with everything he wrote, *L'Ancien Régime et La Révolution* by Alexis de Tocqueville is lucid, engaging, and convincing.

Having cited these authors, I'd like to say that any errors of interpretation on my part are their fault for not expressing themselves clearly, but it wouldn't be true, and all are recommended for anyone seeking a more intellectually rigorous guide.

As with most works of fiction, quite ancillary and seemingly irrelevant reading has fed into the making of this novel, above all the wise essays of Wendell Berry, whose thoughts on limits informed the narrator's conclusions on his way home from Rosas.

Everything else is me . . . except for the rubbish bits. They must be by somebody else.

ACKNOWLEDGMENTS

My thanks to Marty and Judy, for books, breathing, and the best curry house in Frankfurt, to Barbara, a copy editor so acute that she can skewer even the most cunningly dissembled imbecility, and to Gary, who saved me from other manifestations of imbecility.